The Headhunters

A full list of L. Ron Hubbard's
novellas and short stories is provided at the back.

*Dekalogy—a group of ten volumes

L. RON HUBBARD

The Headhunters

GALAXY
PRESS

Published by
Galaxy Press, LLC
7051 Hollywood Boulevard, Suite 200
Hollywood, CA 90028

Printed in the United States of America.

ISBN-10 1-59212-358-9
ISBN-13 978-1-59212-358-2

Library of Congress Control Number: 2007903530

Contents

Stories from Pulp Fiction's Golden Age

A ND it *was* a golden age.

The 1930s and 1940s were a vibrant, seminal time for a gigantic audience of eager readers, probably the largest per capita audience of readers in American history. The magazine racks were chock-full of publications with ragged trims, garish cover art, cheap brown pulp paper, low cover prices—and the most excitement you could hold in your hands.

"Pulp" magazines, named for their rough-cut, pulpwood paper, were a vehicle for more amazing tales than Scheherazade could have told in a million and one nights. Set apart from higher-class "slick" magazines, printed on fancy glossy paper with quality artwork and superior production values, the pulps were for the "rest of us," adventure story after adventure story for people who liked to *read*. Pulp fiction authors were no-holds-barred entertainers—real storytellers. They were more interested in a thrilling plot twist, a horrific villain or a white-knuckle adventure than they were in lavish prose or convoluted metaphors.

The sheer volume of tales released during this wondrous golden age remains unmatched in any other period of literary history—hundreds of thousands of published stories in over nine hundred different magazines. Some titles lasted only an issue or two; many magazines succumbed to paper shortages during World War II, while others endured for decades yet. Pulp fiction remains as a treasure trove of stories you can read, stories you can love, stories you can remember. The stories were driven by plot and character, with grand heroes, terrible villains, beautiful damsels (often in distress), diabolical plots, amazing places, breathless romances. The readers wanted to be taken beyond the mundane, to live adventures far removed from their ordinary lives—and the pulps rarely failed to deliver.

In that regard, pulp fiction stands in the tradition of all memorable literature. For as history has shown, good stories are much more than fancy prose. William Shakespeare, Charles Dickens, Jules Verne, Alexandre Dumas—many of the greatest literary figures wrote their fiction for the readers, not simply literary colleagues and academic admirers. And writers for pulp magazines were no exception. These publications reached an audience that dwarfed the circulations of today's short story magazines. Issues of the pulps were scooped up and read by over thirty million avid readers each month.

Because pulp fiction writers were often paid no more than a cent a word, they had to become prolific or starve. They also had to write aggressively. As Richard Kyle, publisher and editor of *Argosy,* the first and most long-lived of the pulps, so pointedly explained: "The pulp magazine writers, the best of them, worked for markets that did not write for critics or attempt to satisfy timid advertisers. Not having to answer to anyone other than their readers, they wrote about human beings on the edges of the unknown, in those new lands the future would explore. They wrote for what we would become, not for what we had already been."

Some of the more lasting names that graced the pulps include H. P. Lovecraft, Edgar Rice Burroughs, Robert E. Howard, Max Brand, Louis L'Amour, Elmore Leonard, Dashiell Hammett, Raymond Chandler, Erle Stanley Gardner, John D. MacDonald, Ray Bradbury, Isaac Asimov, Robert Heinlein—and, of course, L. Ron Hubbard.

In a word, he was among the most prolific and popular writers of the era. He was also the most enduring—hence this series—and certainly among the most legendary. It all began only months after he first tried his hand at fiction, with L. Ron Hubbard tales appearing in *Thrilling Adventures, Argosy, Five-Novels Monthly, Detective Fiction Weekly, Top-Notch, Texas Ranger, War Birds, Western Stories,* even *Romantic Range.* He could write on any subject, in any genre, from jungle explorers to deep-sea divers, from G-men and gangsters, cowboys and flying aces to mountain climbers, hard-boiled detectives and spies. But he really began to shine when he turned his talent to science fiction and fantasy of which he authored nearly fifty novels or novelettes to forever change the shape of those genres.

Following in the tradition of such famed authors as Herman Melville, Mark Twain, Jack London and Ernest Hemingway, Ron Hubbard actually lived adventures that his own characters would have admired—as an ethnologist among primitive tribes, as prospector and engineer in hostile climes, as a captain of vessels on four oceans. He even wrote a series of articles for *Argosy,* called "Hell Job," in which he lived and told of the most dangerous professions a man could put his hand to.

Finally, and just for good measure, he was also an accomplished photographer, artist, filmmaker, musician and educator. But he was first and foremost a *writer,* and that's the L. Ron Hubbard we come to know through the pages of this volume.

This library of Stories from the Golden Age presents the best of L. Ron Hubbard's fiction from the heyday of storytelling, the Golden Age of the pulp magazines. In these eighty volumes, readers are treated to a full banquet of 153 stories, a kaleidoscope of tales representing every imaginable genre: science fiction, fantasy, western, mystery, thriller, horror, even romance—action of all kinds and in all places.

Because the pulps themselves were printed on such inexpensive paper with high acid content, issues were not meant to endure. As the years go by, the original issues of every pulp from *Argosy* through *Zeppelin Stories* continue crumbling into brittle, brown dust. This library preserves the L. Ron Hubbard tales from that era, presented with a distinctive look that brings back the nostalgic flavor of those times.

L. Ron Hubbard's Stories from the Golden Age has something for every taste, every reader. These tales will return you to a time when fiction was good clean entertainment and the most fun a kid could have on a rainy afternoon or the best thing an adult could enjoy after a long day at work.

Pick up a volume, and remember what reading is supposed to be all about. Remember curling up with a *great story.*

—Kevin J. Anderson

KEVIN J. ANDERSON *is the author of more than ninety critically acclaimed works of speculative fiction, including The Saga of Seven Suns, the continuation of the Dune Chronicles with Brian Herbert, and his* New York Times *bestselling novelization of L. Ron Hubbard's* Ai! Pedrito!

The Headhunters

CHAPTER ONE

Travelers Headed for Trouble

DOWN in the hold of the *King Solomon,* a Polynesian sailor was piling up crates of canned food and humming a little under his breath.

It was cool in the hold, but not so outside in the pounding glare of the equatorial sun which, even this late in the afternoon, was scorching Kieta, Solomon Islands.

A footstep sounded behind the naked sailor and he turned, a grin on his face. Slowly the grin faded, to be replaced by a scowl.

Standing easily in the gloom was a dirty-faced white man of chunky build. In his hand he held a snub nosed .45.

"If it an't Hihi," said the white man. "'Oo would have thought to meet you here?"

"You more better get out," snapped Hihi, straightening up. "If boss comes, he killum plenty along you."

The white man grinned. "'E won't be along, Hihi. I left him passing the time o' day at the club."

Hihi looked uneasily up at the bright square of blue sky which filled the hatch opening. He realized that he was alone aboard the schooner and that this man would show very little mercy if he took it into his head to shoot.

The white man, Punjo Charlie, looked amiable enough except for one eye which jiggled up and down and slid back and forth as though well greased. The other eye, being made of glass, stared steadily ahead. *Punjo* stood for "tough one" in the dialect.

"No," said Punjo Charlie, "'e won't be down for a bit. And I think mybe you'd be so good as to tell me right quick something I want to know about Tom Christian."

Hihi made a stealthy move toward the keen dirk in his belt, but Punjo Charlie raised the gun ever so little and grinned a little harder.

"You went upcountry with Christian, Hihi. 'E found hisself too much gold for one man, him and Larsen. Mybe you'd like to tell me where it was, Hihi. Or mybe you're tired of life. Remember what happened to Larsen, Hihi?"

Hihi looked levelly at the white man, not a little contempt in his brown, handsome face. "Yes, I was with boss, but you no get nothing along me. More better you go before boss knock hell outa you."

"Now see here, Hihi," said Punjo Charlie in a whining drone, "you're mighty fond of life, an't you? I wouldn't want nothink to 'appen to you."

Punjo Charlie stepped slowly forward. Hihi backed up until he was against the damp ribs of the schooner's hold.

Punjo Charlie came on. Hihi suddenly gripped his knife hilt and sprang forward and sideways, weapon upraised, ready to strike.

Punjo looked fat and greasy but he could move like a striking snake. He did not fire, for that would bring down the town upon him. He raised his weapon, caught Hihi's knife and brought the .45 butt crashing down on Hihi's curly hair.

The brown man folded up and sank back, his eyes rolling, a seep of blood coming down his face. Punjo Charlie, with a glance at the hatch overhead, picked up several strands of hemp and lashed Hihi's arms and legs together in such a way that Hihi could not move.

The loyal Polynesian showed no immediate signs of waking up and Punjo Charlie had to resort to a full fire bucket which stood to one side. He sent the contents cascading down over Hihi and stood back, his good eye jiggling from the inert brown man to the hatch.

Hihi came awake slowly and then, with an attempt to leap up, felt the force of his ropes and fell violently back, cursing in several languages.

"You wait," cried Hihi. "Boss kill along you plenty, you bet. I not tell you nothing."

"No?" said Punjo Charlie, grinning evilly. "No?"

Punjo took the dirk and felt its edge. Slowly he leaned over the helpless brown man and drew a small pattern of red lines upon the shrinking chest. Hihi clenched his teeth and said nothing.

"Don't bother you none," said Punjo Charlie in disappointment. "Mybe if I was to hack off an ear careful-like you might like to say something about it. After all, Hihi, it an't nothink hard I wants of you. Just tell me where you left that pool full of gold dust and I'll let you stay right where you are. It an't anythink hard to arsk, Hihi."

"I not tell nothing," snapped Hihi.

Punjo Charlie regretfully took hold of Hihi's ear and fondled it. He tested the edge of his knife, assured himself with a glance that Hihi was not going to talk after all and then, raising the blade, prepared to lop off the ear.

But before the knife could descend, heavy footsteps sounded overhead. Hihi started to cry out. Punjo Charlie slapped half a gunnysack into the open mouth, without any regard for Hihi's feelings in the matter. The sack was crawling with copra bugs.

Overhead, a clear, strong voice said, "Hihi! Where are you, you lazy devil?"

Punjo Charlie moved slowly back behind the stacks of crates until he could no longer be seen in the gloom. The footsteps came close to the hatch and Punjo Charlie raised his .45.

"Hihi!"

Punjo Charlie licked his puffy, greasy lips. That was Tom Christian's voice. Punjo had a score to settle with Tom Christian.

A white-clad man in a sailor cap thrust his shoulders and head over the coaming and yelled, "Hihi! You down there?"

Christian swung himself over the edge and clattered down the ladder. He was a little better than six feet tall and his shoulders were wide and straight. His gray eyes were clear and he had the air about him of a man who knows exactly what he wants to do and exactly how he will do it.

Christian reached the bottom and, stooping his head a little to pass under the crossbeams, looked down the length of the gloomy hold.

"Hihi!"

A slight movement in the darkness caused Christian to turn his head. His sun-dazzled eyes were long in picking up the silhouette of brown on the packs.

"What the devil. . . ."

Christian strode over and yanked the gunny sacking out of Hihi's mouth and started in on the strands of rope.

"Boss," whispered Hihi, "Punjo Charlie . . ."

"If you don't mind, Christian," said Punjo in his whiny voice, looking down the sights of his .45, "if you don't mind, just stand there a bit, old fellow. I wouldn't move none if I was you, Christian."

Christian turned slowly and stared at the dirty, blue-jowled face and the jiggly eye. "You!"

"Ra't you are, Christian. Me, Punjo. Owh, I've been looking forward to this, I can tell you. And how are you feeling, Christian?"

"So you've been looking forward to it, have you?" said Christian, acidly. "Well, so have I. I've been looking for you all over the Solomons. I believe I've got something to say to you, Punjo. Something about my partner, Larsen. Of course you wouldn't know anything about his being murdered, would you?"

"Of course not, Christian."

"Oh, of course not," said Christian, bitterly. "Of course not. You caught Larsen when he went back to clean out that pool and you murdered him."

"Why, Christian," reproved Punjo Charlie. "'Ow could you think of such a thing?"

"I can think it all right. But you made a mistake, didn't

you? You killed him before he could lead you to the place we had placered out. And now you're here, are you? It'll be a long time, me bucko, before you spend any of that gold."

"Do tell," said Punjo. "Now an't that too bad. Beg pardon, Christian, but would you mind sitting down there on those crates for just a moment? Long enough for me to put some rope on you? Hi don't want to kill you, Christian. Mybe maim you a little bit, but not kill you. Dead men," he added with a chuckle, "wasn't never known to talk very much."

"Take my advice," said Christian, "and clear out while you're still in one piece. I might change my mind and knock hell out of you."

"Listen to the brave lad," crowed Punjo. His good eye glittered and grew hard and he bared his teeth and his voice dropped down into a snarl. "So help me, Christian, you've stolen that mine off me and I'm going to get you for that. I've got contacts upcountry, Christian. I know Togu and his Kris and you can't arsk for a better lot of murderers than them. You tell me now and I'll let you go. Mybe I'll even split up with you when I get back. But if you think you can get it, Christian, you're a fool. Set one foot upcountry and I'll kill you."

While he had been talking, the .45 had dropped a notch or two, followed closely by Hihi and Christian. The brown man, silent so far, suddenly yelped, "Hello, Barry!" and stared up at the hatch.

Punjo involuntarily whirled toward the patch of blue sky and as he did, Christian's big fist lashed out and caught him on the point of the jaw.

The blue-snouted automatic went whirling into the

darkness. Punjo Charlie staggered back. Christian tried to vault the high pile of crates and get at him but two of the boxes slid off and tripped him.

Punjo knew he had overstayed his time. With a hasty glance about him, he dived for the ladder and started up. Christian pulled himself out of the crates, and searched feverishly about on the deck for a sign of the gun.

Overhead the patch of blue went out as Punjo slammed and locked the hatch cover.

Christian whipped the ropes off Hihi and then raced forward to the other opening. He could hear Punjo making for the gangway.

Leaping up the ladder three at a time, still swearing, Christian reached the dazzling light of day again. He scanned the dock and saw that Punjo was scuttling down its length.

That was all Christian had eyes for at the minute. He did not notice that three newcomers were now standing below looking in amazement at all this commotion, so incongruous in the sleepy peacefulness of Kieta harbor.

Christian leaped over the side and ten feet down to the worn dock planking and sprinted after Punjo.

That very greasy individual had slipped out of sight as though on a larded chute. Christian looked up and down the rows of iron-roofed warehouses and saw nothing but Melanesians sleeping in the shade.

Breathing hard, Christian came back to the gangway and started up. The spokesman of the party of three touched his arm.

"Beg your pardon, sir," said this worthy gentleman, doffing

his sun helmet (which was very new), "but could you tell me where I could find a man known as Tom Christian? Are you the man?"

Christian turned and looked at the others, his mind still on Punjo Charlie. Dimly he noticed that this gentleman was rather old and gray and had the intent face of a scholar. The second member of the party was a young man of so well-bred an air that Christian knew it could not be true.

When he saw the third, he forgot all about Punjo. The third member was a girl whose eyes were so cool and so calm and so assured that you knew she had a hundred dresses and a dozen maids. She looked like something out of a fairy story in the filmy white dress. You expected her to be royal and imperial and a little bored. Christian found the face so interesting that he stared. Beautiful white women were few and far between in the Solomon Islands. The girl gave him look for look.

"We heard that you were leaving for the hills," continued the old gentleman, "and we thought we might prevail upon you to guide us. We would pay. . . ."

Christian's face suddenly fell into an astonished looseness. "Upcountry?" he said as though he couldn't believe his ears.

"Yes, yes, upcountry."

"You?" said Christian, still not believing it.

"Why . . . why, er, yes, upcountry. You see, I am Professor Forsythe of Hale University. I have been sent out to trace the origin of the Melanesians and Micronesians. This is my assistant, George d'Stuyveseant, and this is my daughter, Diana Forsythe. You *are* Mr. Christian, aren't you?"

Christian nodded, still amazed. "You mean," he said carefully, "that you are going upcountry with these people, this woman, I mean?"

"Why, yes, yes. We've just landed here and we have but little time. I am very anxious to get this work over with, Mr. Christian, because it is so important."

"Did you ever hear of headhunters?" said Christian.

Professor Forsythe brightened instantly. In some excitement he removed his glasses and polished them thoroughly. Then he replaced them, took them off and polished them again.

"Yes, yes," said the professor. "I had heard it and I'm glad to know that you confirm the opinion. There *are* headhunters there, aren't there?" he added hopefully.

If Christian had been surprised before, he was astounded now. He looked them over carefully, one to the others, and blinked two or three times. They were carefully dressed, he saw, and their fingernails were clean, and they looked well fed and soft.

"You mean," said Christian, getting this thing straight once and for all, "you mean you're glad there are headhunters up there?"

"Yes, yes," cried Forsythe. "Yes, yes. You see, if there are headhunters, there will be heads, perhaps left over from the centuries, and if that is true, then I have a chance of proving that these people are not a separate race, but descended from Negritos and Malays, perhaps."

"And you want to go get these heads?" said Christian.

When the professor and the girl and the assistant all nodded as though moved by the same string, Christian suddenly felt a desire to laugh in their faces. These people were just out of the United States, just out of a land where a cop stood on every corner and where you merely snapped your fingers and you had clean clothes and good food and a ride as far as you wanted to go—and they wanted to find the headhunters.

And Christian, wild, arrogant soul that he was, might have laughed if Hihi had not appeared that moment carrying Punjo's .45 automatic.

"You get that son—?" said Hihi.

The girl blushed and looked startled. The assistant bristled a little and then stared wide-eyed at the gun.

"No," said Christian. "Hihi, set something in the cabin for these people." And to the three, he said, "Of course you'll come up and have a spot of something."

Christian had taken the automatic. He spun it about now by the guard as though it was the most natural thing in the world to do.

The professor nudged Christian. "You had better put that away, Mr. Christian. Here comes a man who looks like a police officer."

Christian stared blankly at Forsythe and then turned to welcome the khaki-clad young Australian who swung jauntily up the dock.

"Hello, Barry," said Christian. "You're late."

"Yes, damn it," said Barry with a smile. "I heard Punjo Charlie had been down here raising the devil. Hallo, Professor, beastly hot, isn't it?"

Forsythe looked from the gun to Barry and then realized

that its presence had no significance to the police lieutenant. This was a startling fact to Forsythe. He had just come from a country where the possession of firearms meant a year or so in jail.

The realization struck all three of them and some of their ease of manner deserted them. The girl moved away.

"It's terribly warm," she drawled. "I am sure Mr. Christian will excuse us. Come along, Father, I think these gentlemen have some business."

"But . . . but . . ." sputtered Forsythe.

George d'Stuyveseant and the girl were already walking away. The professor followed them.

In an awed voice, Christian said to Barry, *"They're going upcountry."*

"They've got as much right to get killed as the next," drawled Barry, swinging his swagger cane.

"You can't let them go," said Christian. "It's murder."

"The resident must be drunk. He said they could. But see here, Tom, old chap, you can't do this, you know."

"Do what?"

Barry shook his head. "You can't go upcountry with Punjo Charlie itching for your hide. I won't let you get killed that way. He has Togu and the Kri tribe out. I know. He fools them with that beastly glass eye, you know. Fancy that, now. A glass eye."

"Listen," said Christian, "he had a hand in killing Larsen. I know that. Well, I can't let him scare me out. There's a half million at stake."

"You're a stubborn blighter," said the Australian. "As

13

stubborn as these countrymen of yours, Tom. Give up this thing right now before you're dead and leave your head hanging in a long house up in those hills."

This was a long speech for Lieutenant Barry, but Christian was not impressed. "He can't scare me out. He killed Larsen and I've got that to attend to. Besides, I've waited too long now. I couldn't go with Larsen earlier, and that's why it happened."

"I can't go with you," said Barry. "Not for another week."

"And then the rains will start. I've got to get up there before Punjo Charlie does, the filthy scum. I've got to get there and out before he can, and I'm leaving as soon as I can get things together."

Barry sighed and followed Christian into the cabin.

CHAPTER TWO

Grim Warning to Christian

CHRISTIAN, dressed in a white mess jacket with silver buttons and black tuxedo pants, walked swiftly along the dark streets of Kieta that night, heading for the club where he knew he would find the professor. He told himself that he wanted to discourage them in going up into the hills, but that did not account for his careful dress. He kept thinking of the girl, Diana.

As he passed a narrow side street lined with thatched huts, he did not see a blot of dirty white against the wall and did not hear what that blot said.

"Owh, if it an't Christian," whispered Punjo Charlie to himself, grinning ghoulishly. "All dressed up wiv his bib and tucker and going to see the young lydy. So *that's* the way the wind blows, is it? Ah, young love, how pretty it is. Two young doves . . ." He paused and snickered to himself, gazing at Christian's retreating and unconscious back. "'E won't tell me where it is, will he? And 'e won't have nothink to do with me. And he thinks mybe 'e can tyke a machine gun upcountry wiv him. Owh, what a brave bloke, Mr. Christian. Wot a brave bloke! And young love, too. Mybe if I scare him a bit 'e won't be so brave. And mybe if anythink was to 'appen to the young lydy, 'e'd come a-runnin' to 'er aid, bless 'er. Mybe that gives me an idea, Mr. Christian. Mybe you an't done

15

your best before, but you'll 'ave to do it now or my nyme an't Punjo." He turned back to a black Melanesian behind him and whispered some orders.

Christian, without knowing anything of this, went up the steps of the club and found the three Americans already attended upon by Barry.

Diana's bored look brightened when Christian appeared. George d'Stuyveseant—who was responsible for the engagement ring on Diana's hand—scowled darkly. The professor pursued his talk with Barry.

"And so," said the professor, "when this man Gregory brought out a book and called me a liar, I knew that I had to prove it to him by coming out and finding these heads. The honor of Hale is at stake, Mr. Barry."

"Let it stand that way," said Christian, motioning Pete the barman to bring him a neat one. "You can't go up there, Forsythe. It's not safe."

"He has me along," said George, frowning and affecting an English accent.

Christian looked at George's soft hands. The girl Diana had not even heard George. She was fascinated by Christian's broad shoulders and tan face.

Christian might have gone on had it not been for footsteps on the verandah. He looked up and saw a fuzzy-headed hillman entering, carrying a package. The man, naked except for a loincloth, came stolidly across the room.

"Hiyou, you come along what fellah?" Christian wanted to know.

The native had no answer for that. He gave Christian the box.

Christian took it thoughtlessly and spread the leaves apart to reveal a basket of woven grass which he promptly upended.

Diana shrieked and fell back. George gurgled and looked green. Barry clucked his tongue while Christian turned the thing over.

It was about the size of a man's fist and it had no eyes, only sockets. Its hair was blond and matted with blood. It was an incredibly shrunken, parchment-dry human head.

"Larsen," said Christian, his knuckles getting very white.

Suddenly Christian was on his feet and the table was upset and the human head was rolling with a drum sound across the black polished floor.

Christian's big hands had the native by the shoulders. Christian roared, "Who sent that, you ——?"

The native let out a shrill yelp of terror.

Christian's open palm on the native's face sounded like a cannon shot. "Who sent it?"

Again the native yelled and Christian threw the fellow halfway across the room. The hurtling body crashed into wicker chairs and sent them spinning in their turn.

With long, deadly strides, Christian was upon the man again. Christian's big palms cracked against the flesh.

"Who sent it?"

"Look out!" roared Barry. "Look out, he's got a knife!"

The native came up with a war cry, steel flickering in the light—steel which was artistically smeared with poison.

Christian's big hands had the native by the shoulders.
Christian roared, "Who sent that, you ——?"

Christian dropped to one side and tried to get at his shoulder holster. The silver buttons were too faithful to their task and would not break. The knife came down in a vicious, glinting arc.

The room was drowned in the roar of a Colt .45. The native staggered and flung out his arms. The knife tinkled when it skittered across the polished black wood. The native stumbled forward with thick blood drooling between his set black teeth. He thumped down and his palms patted the planking in three measured beats. Then he lay still.

Pete laid the .45 down on the bar. Smoke still curled from the muzzle. Pete came around through the trap and walked stiffly toward Christian. Pete bore a neat whiskey in his hand although no one had seen him pour it. He thrust it into Christian's fingers.

"Thanks," said Christian in a faint voice. "Here's to you, Pete."

Barry scooped Larsen's cured head into the basket again and set it on the table. Then he walked to the bar and cranked the phone.

"Send up a wagon for a dead hillman," said Barry. "The club, right. No, no trouble."

Christian walked back to the table and carefully set down the glass. His hand was very steady. "Sorry," he said briefly to the three dead white faces which stared at him.

Barry looked out on the verandah and loosened his shoulder gun in its spring holster just in case. "That's a warning," said Barry. "Better not leave in the morning, Tom."

19

"Of course I'll leave in the morning," said Christian.

"No, listen," begged Barry. "Listen. Punjo Charlie must have sent that thing down here. I told you he killed Larsen. Now doesn't that prove it?"

"Punjo wouldn't cure a white man's head," said Christian.

"No? The devil you say. That's what he did and it's a warning not to clean out that pool."

"What if it is?" demanded Christian. "No man is going to do me out of half a million bucks. He's scared of me or he wouldn't have tried this warning."

"Listen," pleaded Barry, "I know you're walking into certain death. Don't leave in the morning. Wait a week and I'll go with you."

"Can't. Got to get in and out before the rain. Can't clean that pool in the rain."

Barry turned back to the native and stirred him with the toe of his boot to make sure he was really dead and not shamming. Barry did it absently, his mind busy with other things.

The professor came to life unexpectedly. "But that . . . but that isn't a native head, Mr. Christian. That looked like a white man's head. I came up here for native heads they told me I could get in the long houses. You see, a man by the name of Gregory—Professor Gregory—published, at his expense, a pamphlet which . . ."

Christian wasn't listening to him. "When your men come, get that Baptist minister down here and we'll bury what's left of Larsen, poor devil."

"Right," said Barry and went to the wall phone.

George helped Diana out of her chair, but he looked worse

off than she did. His face had a puttylike quality which took all the well-bred dignity away.

Christian gave Diana a short bow. "I'm sorry, Miss Forsythe. I didn't—"

"I am sure you didn't," said Diana, bitterly, looking all the way through him. "I'm sure you didn't."

"Uncouth ruffian," muttered George, tottering away.

Barry gave Christian a startled glance and they both shrugged a little.

"You see, Mr. Christian," said the professor, "I must have the material. . . ."

CHAPTER THREE

Jungle Prey

T HE mists which hung about the peaks looked like false
cotton beards upon an already hairy face. Rain came
and washed the steep hillsides and then the sun came and
dried them out again. But down in the tunnels which passed
for paths through the jungle it was always wet, always hot,
always muddy.

The bold headlands of the coast were far behind, the
pleasant valleys lay ahead, and the Forsythe "Expedition"
coiled along the craggy slopes in anticipation of level, cooler
ground. The ground would be slightly more even, of course,
but not any cooler, as the large island lay a scant six degrees
below the equator.

A horse, of sorts, had fallen to George's lot and as a
consequence, George's temper was something to behold. It
was impossible to ride on these narrow paths, and instead of
the horse carrying George, George was carrying the horse—or
so it seemed to that very hot, very sweaty, very rumpled young
man.

George had read a lot about these islands and he understood
that it was customary for Western men to be carried on
palanquins—or maybe that was Cochin China. He had also
read that a horse was handy in steep places because you could

hold his tail and let him take you as a towboat takes a liner. But George's horse, being very gnawed by ticks and such and being generally out of sorts, refused, with a few deft heel stabs, to tow anything, and besides, the trees and branches had fallen in some recent typhoon and the mount had some difficulty in negotiating the rotting windfalls.

Diana trudged disconsolately, realizing that the boots which were so picturesque in the shop windows of Fifth Avenue had never been intended for walking at all. She had used three rolls of adhesive tape and they were only three days upon their way and her heels were getting steadily worse. It was not, furthermore, very ladylike to be so moist, and powder became glue when applied to a damp nose. Her well-tailored khaki was plastered with red mud where she had fallen and, partly because of her appearance, she felt very depressed, trudging there in the line of sweating native bearers.

Only the professor seemed to be enjoying himself. He carried a big camera under his frail arm and he beamed intently at all inanimate objects as though telling each one, "Hello, glad to see you."

Forsythe did not mind the flies, the mosquitoes, the mud and the rotting windfalls simply because he did not have time to notice them at all. It was therefore with surprise that he discovered the temper of his two young assistants, but even that did not dampen the professor's interest in botany, jungle biology, geology and humanology. His bearers fascinated him, the trees were his friends, the bright-eyed lizards were quite cheerful, and even the flies reminded him that the government

24

might do well to import a certain Japanese species which would eat this species up. He must tell that to the resident. Yes, indeed, he must tell that to the resident.

It was with astonishment that the professor found his way blocked by a short, squatty black Melanesian who was not at all cheerful and who was most horribly tattooed. The professor stopped abruptly and as he was in the lead, the whole party, unable to pass in this narrow defile, stopped with him; albeit there was much bumping and three or four loads were spilled and George tripped over a bearer and went down into the muck to come up somewhat blacker than when he went down.

"How do you do?" said the professor, politely.

"Them fellah b'long along you?" demanded the tattooed obstruction.

"Oh, yes," said Forsythe, scrubbing at his square glasses and replacing them. "Oh, yes, indeed."

"Ummmmmmmmm."

"Beg pardon?"

"Coast man," said the obstruction. "All b'long coast man. No can do along hillman."

"Yes, yes, to be sure. What did you say?"

Here a very important member of the Forsythe "Expedition" thrust his way to the fore. He was dressed in extremely white clothes and he carried a small stick and his hair was cut short. He was an educated Melanesian, one who had affected white man's dress and customs and who considered himself far too good for either black or white. His name was Banjo, but he insisted upon the Mister from one and all.

25

"Hey!" said Mister Banjo, threatening the tattooed obstruction with his frail stick. "You get out." With another motion of the stick he made it emphatic in dialect.

The hillman looked curiously at the stick and the black man in white clothes. The hillman's eyes grew very, very calculating as though he measured this fellah for a couple pork roasts. He licked his lips.

Another outburst from Mister Banjo occasioned the obstruction no worry whatever. Mister Banjo used his swagger stick as though it was a baton and as though he directed a dozen symphony orchestras, his voice as shrill as the wailing violins.

"Get out!" yelled Banjo.

Methodically, the obstruction took the swagger stick out of Banjo's astonished hand and slowly broke it in four sections across his bony knee, tossing it into the brush.

"Coast man no can do," said the tattooed one. His fingers twitched a little as though they might like the feel of trade goods or perhaps money.

Mister Banjo's rage had reached its height and had cracked and had left him quite nerveless. He stood defensively behind the professor.

It occurred to Forsythe, then, that a tattooed man in the hills meant that that man had had considerable success in battle and was credited with killing a few men.

George shoved a bearer and Mister Banjo out of the way and blustered up beside the professor. "What's the matter with this savage?"

"Now, George," said Forsythe, "I wouldn't say that. He might be sensitive, you know. He says he won't allow these coast men to come into his hills."

"Give him some money or some beads or something," snapped George, very brave with his hand upon the butt of a Smith & Wesson .25 automatic.

"Please, George," said Diana, coming up. "Don't do anything to get hurt."

"I'll take care of this," said George, setting his jaw for Diana's benefit. He reached out and gave the obstruction a tap on the chest. "Get out of the way, my man."

The Melanesian moved back, the better to look this white one over, but George took it as a retreat. He gave the fellow a harder tap on the chest. Again the man moved backward. George was suddenly filled with a lion's courage, and with a mighty shove, sent the Melanesian hurtling into the mud.

Abruptly they heard a twanging sound in the brush and a whipping rush of air over their heads. Behind them the lead bearer shrieked and dropped his load to clutch at his naked black chest.

The feathered shaft of an arrow protruded there, making a thin rivulet of blood which mingled with the glistening globes of sweat. Fingers clawing at it, the bearer slid to the ground, doubled up and writhing. Suddenly he lay still.

Diana staggered against George and stared in horror at the surrounding denseness of the jungle.

Professor Forsythe wiped his glasses and said, "Dear me, dear me, how unfortunate."

George looked down at his hand and then at the native's chest and became a little green about the mouth.

The bearers were bunched up about Mister Banjo, who had somehow retreated, weasel-like, through the press.

On every side, bushes began to move and slitted-black eyes and bushy, enormous heads of hair appeared. The tattooed one had not changed his expression in any way whatever. He did not even look at the dead man; he was studying George with an odd fascination. Once he reached out and felt George's arm much as one feels a steak to see if it is tender, and then for some reason he licked his thick, protruding lips.

The hillmen in the bushes moved in, reducing their circle, hands ready upon bowstrings and arrows affixed. There was not a single expression in the lot. They were twoscore robots moving jerkily and efficiently without command. When they had taken up their positions they stood very still, like so many black leopards waiting for a victim to pass under their tree limb.

Diana could not make a sound. Some strange, stiff fluid ran through her body and turned her into an ice statue. She felt very alone and very afraid and she knew that when this was over she would cry, but just now she could do nothing but stare.

"Dear me," said Forsythe, polishing his glasses on his shirttail. "Dear me."

There was a stir up the trail and they could hear a man coming toward them, his boots squishing as he walked through the red mud. They waited and the Melanesians waited and the bearers stilled their chattering teeth.

It seemed like the fellow came forever, but all of a sudden he was there, standing before the professor, grinning.

"Hallo there," said Punjo Charlie affably. "Hallo. 'Ad a nice trip?"

"Oh, oh yes," said Forsythe, seriously. "I . . . perhaps you know these gentlemen."

"Know them?" said Punjo Charlie, looking all about him with some surprise. "Why, yes, I seem to recognize some of them."

"Well . . . er . . . would you mind telling them to go away?"

"Go away? Them chaps? Right-ho." Punjo Charlie waved his hand at them and said, "Go away."

The hillmen moved silently back into the brush, and outside of the tattooed one, they had thoroughly disappeared in less than ten seconds. But they were still there and the effect was worse than before. Before you could see them, but now an arrow might come any instant as it had a few minutes ago.

Punjo Charlie was most hearty and very cordial. His one eye remained steadily looking straight ahead, but the other was squinted and roved back and forth a great deal. His round sharkskin face was more stubbly and bluer than before and his clothes—boots and khaki pants and a once-white shirt—were a little dirtier, if possible. He kept rubbing his thick, unnaturally white hands together as though he had them in soap and water.

"Well, well, well," said Punjo Charlie.

"Oh, yes," said Forsythe. "Yes, indeed."

"An't it a small world?" said Punjo Charlie.

29

"Oh, yes," said the professor.

"Well, well, well," commented the renegade again, but it was seen that he made no move to let them reform and pass up the trail. He turned toward Diana and let his squinted eye whisk up and down and sideways a few times and then rubbed his hands some more. After a little he looked her over a second series of times and then belatedly tipped his grubby, half-melted pith helmet to her.

"And 'ow are you, missee?" said Punjo Charlie.

Diana could only nod weakly, fascinated by his motionless, guileless eye and its violent contrast to his shifty, active orb. George had somehow slipped out of their ken and might as well have been a muddy blot of fungus on the log where he sat.

Receiving no enlightening answer, Punjo Charlie turned again to the professor. "My, my, an't she the shy one though?"

"Oh, yes," said Forsythe. "Yes, indeed."

"I s'y," said Punjo Charlie, "look at those boxes and such. Anything in them that's be hurt by the mud? They left a frightful mess."

Forsythe and Diana looked back along the muddy path and saw with a start that they had not one single bearer left. Somehow the fellows had evaporated and, it would seem, had become a part of the straggly mist which clung in the twilight of the trees.

The baggage was strewn everywhere and, because of fright, was still intact. The bearers would rather take their lives with them than a heavy load.

Punjo Charlie grinned placidly at them all, scrubbed his

hands some more and then moved down to the baggage. He carefully opened each box and looked within. He saw microscopes and books and small cartons ready for specimens and then, what was really interesting, a considerable quantity of trade goods in the way of beads and mirrors and such.

"Not much," said Punjo Charlie, coming back, his left eye dancing with delight and his right eye very calm, "but you can't expect everything in this world of ours. I often says to me old lady when she was up here with me—though she couldn't speak English none to talk about—that you has to be content with such as God gives you and leave grumblin' to them as 'asn't a free and hopen mind."

"Dear me, yes," said Forsythe, polishing his glasses again.

Punjo Charlie looked at him intently and then, in an apologetic sort of whine, said, "I s'y, you can't do that, you know."

"Er . . . er . . . what?"

"Stop scrubbin' at the bloody things. You can't do that."

"Dear me," said Forsythe, affixing his spectacles to his nose in a great hurry. "I . . . I can't see why—"

"Ow, you can't. Now look here, I'm a good man and I'm a considerate cove as you ever wants to put your peepers on, but blimey, you can't do that 'ere."

With a solemn shake of his head, Punjo Charlie's fingers darted to his right eye, did something very quick, drew a dirty handkerchief from his dirty pants and began to do some polishing himself.

The professor looked on with great interest. The natives

rustled and buzzed for a moment in the brush. The tattooed man in the trail fell away and made some magic signs before his face just in case.

Punjo Charlie was carefully cleaning his glass eye.

After a bit he put it back and turned to the brush. He rattled something in dialect and then turned back to Forsythe with a benign grin.

"I'm a 'elpful cove, y'know. 'Ere you went and lost your coast men and 'ere I am givin' you the pick of the hillmen wiv my compliments."

The Melanesians came slowly out of the brush and hoisted up the baggage without comment.

Forsythe said, "Dear me, but that's thoughtful of you."

"Oh, I thinks of everything. I even got a nice camp for you up the way a bit, and 'oo says I an't kind when I tells you I won't even lock you up none to speak about."

George looked startled and Diana gasped. Punjo Charlie dragged the corpse by its arm and removed it from trail to brush and then, scrubbing his hands and beaming, turned to Diana.

"Not 'arf, not 'arf," said Punjo Charlie. "An't she a beauty though?"

As he addressed none of them, none of them answered. His left eye trailed up and down Diana's slim body and he chuckled in delight.

"Not 'arf," he repeated. "It an't often we sees 'em that sweet down 'ere in this 'ole, I'll tell you. Now there was Chief Chanki's daughter what was ra't nice, but she didn't fancy stayin' so long and kilt herself. Gorblimey, Punjo, but Gord A'mighty certainly looks atter you sometimes."

Feet began to squish in the mud and the natives began to move. George trudged slowly, head down, his horse completely forgotten. Forsythe muttered, "Dear me," from time to time. Diana was shuddering and trying not to cry.

Punjo Charlie treated them to a ballad he had learned, he said, in Singapore. It was fortunate that the others were too downcast to listen.

CHAPTER FOUR

The Road to Revenge

FROM valley to valley, from mountain to mountain, rolled the sound, its own echo building, rolling, vibrating, growling until the island itself shivered down deep in the sea.

"*Rrrroww! Rrrrroh!*" thundered the drums.

Not a beat, not a single sound. The concentration of a hundred skin heads racking themselves to pieces against the wall of night.

Dots of fire glittered up against the stars, studding the lowering wall of the hills where the villages crowded together on stilts.

"*Rrrroww! Rrrrrroh!*"

The drums had rolled that way for the Spanish conquerors, for the French conquerors, for the Italian conquerors, for the Portuguese conquerors. And all of these were dead and yet the drums still growled and roared and bellowed out their messages.

Tom Christian stared into his fire, his lean features painted by shadow and flame, his eyes seeing deep into the coals and perhaps reading a warning there.

"Hell of a row," said Christian.

His four Polynesians, statuesque men of brown from the *King Solomon*, crouched on their haunches across from him, their eyes reflecting the flame.

35

"Too much," said Hihi, the wisest and strongest of the four. "Last time, he don't yell like them yell."

"No," said Christian. "That's what I'm afraid of. It can't be us."

Christian thought it over for a long time. He had come from a point south of the main trail, well knowing the folly of trying to enter the valleys in the usual way. He had been on the trail for four days.

"I wonder if those fool people left after we did," said Christian.

"No can read drums," said Hihi.

"Bah, the drums. The drums. If I ever hear another drum . . ." Christian looked out into the darkness. His hand moved swiftly and threw his khaki coat away from the sub-tommy. He stood up slowly, very intent upon a new and strange noise which had floated to his keen ears. The Polynesians skipped quietly backwards into the dark. A rattle told Christian that they had rifles in their hands.

A strange figure moved in toward them. It was white and black, and it staggered.

"Banjo," muttered Christian.

"That's right, I'm Banjo. I'm good man, don't shoot— I'm Banjo."

Christian looked him over. The fellow had come far. The knees of his once stiffly starched pants were completely gone and the suit of which he had been so proud was now nothing but a limp remnant. He came closer to the fire and cast a shivering glance back into the darkness he had left.

Christian dropped the machine gun and grabbed Banjo's

arm. "I get it, damn you. You were to guide those people and you've sold them out. Where are they?"

The grip was stronger than Christian realized. It sent white agony shooting up Banjo's arm and made him drop to his knees. He groveled before the white man. "I don't sell nothing out. One big feller with a thousand natives jumped us and we fought for three hours and then when everybody was killed I had to get away, but they were so—"

"I want the truth," said Christian, quietly.

"The big feller got an eye that jumps out from his face. He—"

"Uh-huh, Punjo Charlie. Where did they take them?"

"I don't know, I don't know."

"Didn't wait to find out, that it?"

"He had two thousand—"

Christian dropped the man's arm and stood back with his hands on his hips, contempt making hard lines in his face. "Brave Mister Banjo," said Christian. "Banjo the fire-eater. So you ran off and left them after you'd run them into an ambush. And you knew what would happen to them, didn't you? You knew. Oh, yes, you did. They'll take their heads and dry them and they'll eat their flesh." Christian pushed Banjo over with his foot. "You yellow—!"

Hihi came up with an idea of his own. "Lemme kill'm."

"No," said Christian. "Listen, me brave bucko, what village took them?"

Banjo was weeping, perhaps from relief at being comparatively safe. He cared nothing, just now, for his haughty pride. He had learned to wear and discard it at will.

"Little fellah, all striped. Plenty big warrior."

37

Christian nodded. "Where?"

"Tiki Pass."

"Anybody killed?"

"One fellah."

"Lemme kill'm," said Hihi, wistfully fingering his machete.

"No," said Christian, absently. He walked back and forth before the flames and kicked thoughtfully at the turf. Once in a while he turned and looked out into the darkness.

"What time today?" said Christian.

"This morning, plenty early," blubbered Banjo.

"Uh-huh. That's the Kri men. That's Chief Togu. Uh-huh. Hell of a chance I've got. . . ."

He walked back and forth again, stopping more frequently to look at the darkness and listen to the vibrations which rolled and rumbled.

Finally he did not walk at all. "Damn that Punjo Charlie. I should have killed him. Yes, I should have killed him deader'n hell when I had the chance. Scum. If I go . . ."

Hihi came closer. "White missee plenty good, boss. We come to clean pool but we kill'm plenty hillmen, huh?"

Christian turned and looked at him, wondering at the ancient hatred which had always kept brown coast men at the throat of the hillmen. Hihi was more than anxious to go.

But the decision had two sides to it. It wasn't just a half million in gold which had brought Tom Christian into the upcountry. It was a sort of revenge against all the hillmen and Punjo Charlie.

Lars Larsen, rawboned Swede, had been Christian's partner for years on a dozen different enterprises. The two of them

38

had spent three months at the source of a stream, placering down a bank which glittered with dust. It had been hard, dangerous work—hydraulic all day and then kill headhunters all night. But before they could clean their riffles in the stream below, even though the dust which had been caught there on copper plates was worth considerably more than five hundred thousand, the rains had come and the stream had risen twelve feet overnight. Not being deep-sea divers, either of them, and having no other alternative, they had left the scene.

At the start of the next dry season, some six months before, Lars had contacted Christian and had sent a message stating that he was going to have a try for the dust again. But Christian had been too busy and too far away to come back immediately and Lars, in his impatience, had not waited.

And the blond head had come that evening in the small wicker basket, a present from the grim hills.

Revenge was more important to Christian than the half million. Far more important. Christian was a sort of conquistador, followed by the pick of fighting men as were these four. They shared in any loot such as this stream full of dust. Openhanded Christian had made fortunes before. The money had gone but he still had his friends.

"You think I no like kill'm?" said Hihi.

Christian picked up the sub-tommy and barked a command at his coast man bearers. Shadows scuttled through the night, back and forth across the fire.

In less than fifteen minutes the camp was struck and packed. Christian prodded Banjo to his feet.

"I'm sure," said Christian, "that this was Togu and the Kri

village, but you're going to lead me back to the point where you were jumped. Understand?"

Banjo shivered and looked on the verge of tears, but he moved out with Christian behind him and the bearers following.

"More better lemme kill'm," pleaded Hihi. "Them fellah no good."

"March along," said Christian, machine gun nestling beneath his arm.

They marched along the muddy black trail for hours. Once or twice they caught sight of villages but they skirted them in silence. It was hard going, toilsome work in the blackness, but Christian knew that this was their only chance of being left alone. He did not want to fight half the villages in the section just to get to the main scene of action.

Through his mind flitted the picture of Diana leaning back in her wicker chair at the club. Yes, he guessed she was worth saving, even though that fellow George something-or-other had his name up for son-in-law election. After all, you had to stick by your own kind, and if you didn't, then there'd be hell to pay.

A small voice way back in his handsome head whispered, "You think that girl is pretty swell, don't you?"

"No," said Christian. "She needs a licking."

"But she's a looker and she could be very nice if—"

"Shut up," said Christian.

"Bah," said the small voice, "you can't fool me. You think you're a knight-errant going out to save the lady faire. She'll just look down her nose and sniff at you."

"Yeah, but look what's happening to the poor kid. If that lunk Punjo so much as—"

"She isn't yours to protect."

"And what if I make her mine to protect?"

The voice was stilled.

After five dreary black hours of trail they came upon a bright dot in the jungle. They could see the thin slivers of light coming through a stockade wall ahead of them and the partial silhouette of a man squatting over a barrel-like drum. Hands kneaded the instrument and black sound roared across the black hills.

Christian thrust Banjo back into the mass of his men and stepped forward.

A glance at the east told him that the sun was almost there. The sky was plated by a long streak of mother-of-pearl. The stars were already pale and the drummer still drummed. Yes, this must be the village which harbored Punjo Charlie and his captives. Perhaps . . . perhaps that girl was already . . .

Christian tucked the butt of the sub-tommy under his arm and pressed the trigger.

The shrill rataplan made the night shiver, cutting off and annihilating the bellow of the drum, sending the drummer hurtling into cover.

Lead fists began to shake the gate, metal teeth beavered the poles and made the splinters fly.

"Punjo!" yelled Christian. "Come out, you son, or by God, I'll kill every so-and-so in your lousy compound!"

CHAPTER FIVE

Punjo's Trap — and Ultimatum

A palm frond clattered in the morning wind. The fire leaped higher and higher as though frightened, and painted the sides of the shacks on stilts and showed them up in their shabbiness.

"Punjo!" roared Christian again. He could see but little in the gloom and the fire hindered rather than helped, making shadows move where nothing moved at all.

Christian knew better than to stride into the compound and invite a shrill chorus of arrows. He turned and said to Hihi, "Where's that Banjo?"

Hihi asked the question again. Nobody had seen Banjo and nobody knew what had happened to him.

"Devil," said Christian. "He's run away again."

Once more he stared into the compound through the demolished gate. Only one thing for it. He had to walk forward and see what he could and stop archers before they stopped him.

It was an eerie entrance. The village was dead but the fire was alive. The silence of the night was so intense that it hurt the ears as badly as had the now silent and abandoned drum.

Christian's boots were silent on the soft ground. He walked stiffly and his face was hard and impassive.

The first hut was empty. Warily he approached a second.

43

Only one thing for it. He had to walk forward and see what he could and stop archers before they stopped him.

It too was deserted. Christian looked about him with a sense of bewilderment. He had expected to fight, had expected hand-to-hand killing, and now . . .

A yell of agony lashed at him from the line of his bearers. In the darkness he could barely see the man fall. A shrill whipping sound immediately followed from the dense jungle behind the motionless party.

Christian whirled and began to run out of the village toward his men and bearers. He knew what had happened. He had been allowed to pass through an ambush of headhunters. Word had gone ahead by unseen scouts. The headhunters had deserted their village to wait for them in the jungle.

Christian yelled, "Hihi! Get the men into the village! It's empty!"

With a rush the coast men fled in terror away from the death which came winging its way out of the thick undergrowth, and made for the gate, passing Christian.

At least they had the village for protection, thought Christian, looking for Hihi. The brown man came running back with his three brothers in race.

Hihi pointed back toward the path from whence the party had come. "Them fellahs out there. Thousands of 'em!"

"Get into the village," ordered Christian. "It's empty."

Christian covered their retreat with a few bursts from the tommy gun. Arrows were whipping out of the trees, hitting the stockade wall until it looked as though a porcupine hide had been stretched there.

Christian backed into the compound and saw that his whole party was inside. Hihi slammed the gate into place.

Christian looked bleakly about him and then grinned. He had meant to catch the headhunters here and now they had shifted and caught him instead.

The coast men found refuge in the biggest hut and disappeared. They had not been there a minute before they saw the heads, some yawning, some laughing, some sad. Heads, swinging back and forth, looking like so many baseballs or clock pendulums. All dried, shrunken, carefully cured and saved. But the coast men knew it too late and could now only moan in petrified fear. Perhaps these were their brothers, long disappeared, or their fathers or their friends.

Christian looked toward the back of the stockade and saw that he might effect a breach and retreat before they could be surrounded. He made a move toward it and the arrows flew thick about him.

They were penned in this flimsy structure like so many blackbirds in a big cage. Christian was perplexed. It was not likely that the Kris had heard of his coming in time to get out every chicken and child in the place, but they had done so and had carefully laid an ambush on the trail which had failed to materialize only because Christian and the sub-tommy led the van.

This was the village he wanted. He knew that now. But where were the Americans? That girl and Punjo? Angrily Christian marched back to the gate. If he could make his men get out of here, he himself could clear the path with the machine gun. And even in that there was plenty of risk.

If he got out he would have to leave the coast men. They would not follow him because their terror was too great.

Damn them for cowards. He could not leave their heads in the long house.

A voice filtered through the stockade poles, and in the misty grayness of the as yet unborn dawn Christian could see a vague figure detach itself from the jungle, carrying a white rag on a crooked pole.

It was Punjo Charlie, as unwholesome as ever. He swaggered quite a bit because he knew he held the winning hand. A triumphant smile lit up his face but could not dispel the gray blueness of his jowl.

"Owh there, Christian," said Punjo Charlie. "Look here, I've got a truce, y'know."

"Beat it before I plug you," said Christian through the gate.

"Now that an't kind, Christian. Be a gentleman, old chap. You an't a bad cove when you try. I've come wiv a most reasonable request to myke."

Christian knew better than to expose himself to hidden archers in this growing light. Punjo Charlie was not past such tricks.

"Make it fast," said Christian. "I ought to plug you now and save myself the trouble later."

"Don't be so fighty, old chap. I've got a ra'ht good amount of news for you."

"Well?"

"The old gent, y'know, is 'appy as a cat in a milkhouse, Christian. 'E says 'e wouldn't know what to do wivout me. The man needs a bit of a lesson, don't you think? 'E's dreadful spoiled. And the young lydy, Christian, is just as merry as can be. You don't want to hurt them, do you?"

"Get it over," said Christian.

"The young lydy, now, is a pretty little thing, an't she, Christian? Since Chief Chanki's bit o' muslin died, I've been pretty lonesome-like. Now you wouldn't want anything to happen to the young lydy, would you, Christian?"

Christian patted the butt of the sub-tommy.

Punjo Charlie was not the least bit abashed. He was grinning in righteous warmth, shedding good-fellowship all about him. "And the ole man, Christian. 'E an't so strong and 'e's pretty thinlike, but 'e'd 'oller somethin' terrible if we was to toast 'im a bit."

Punjo saw that Christian was still listening and, fixing his good eye upon the sub-tommy and keeping it quiet thereby, he went on.

"Now the young bucko, Christian, is pretty fatlike. 'E would myke a tysty morsel, Togu tells me, and Togu is getting a bit impatient, waiting for me to myke up his mind. Besides, 'is head would be a pretty thing to see a-hangin' from a beam, smiling and good-natured like. Now, Christian, you wouldn't want all that on your conscience, would you?"

"What's the answer?" snarled Christian.

"I'll tell you, old chap. It's a mighty simple sort of thing I'm arsking you to do. That gent Larsen was most provokin', not wantin' to tell me where that pool was 'id. And the nytives has some 'azy notion about it but they can't just exactly say because, when it rained, you know, the vines growed down over everything in 'orrible confusion.

"Now, if you was a reasonable gent like I thinks you be,

48

you'll just give me some hidea of 'ow far that place is from 'ere and I'll pop over there and find out if you're right."

"I see," said Christian, his face very hard. "You think you've got the ace card, that it? You think you can . . . Listen here, Punjo Charlie, I'll give you some good advice. When I kill you I'll see to it personally that your head is left to hang in a long house. I'll give you my solemn word upon it and my word is always good."

Punjo Charlie grinned at him but his good eye jiggled quite a bit.

"I'll tell you where it is," said Christian, "if you'll bring me those three people unharmed, right now. My word is good, you know that."

"It an't much of a promise," said Punjo Charlie, "because you see, I'll take all of you back—and probably roast all of you alive—except the young lydy—if it an't where you said it was. And don't think, Christian, that you can 'ammer your bleedin' w'y out of 'ere, because I've got three villages all around you and I told them that there was plenty to be 'ad in your packs."

Christian knew what Punjo Charlie's word was worth, but he believed the part about the villages and he believed that it was up to him, gold or no gold, to get the others and himself out of here. Punjo Charlie would hardly let them get back to the coast under any condition after this.

Swaggering, but shrugging once in a while as though he felt bullets scratching his back, Punjo went back toward the jungle.

CHAPTER SIX

The Troublesome Prisoners

IT was full daylight when the captives were brought into the stockade. They were trussed on long poles like so many spitted oxen ready for the barbecue pit. They were all limp and haggard and they did not know what was happening to them until they saw Christian. Then something like relief appeared in their eyes.

Punjo Charlie was there at the gate to receive his directions. Christian handed him a slip of paper with a map drawn upon it.

"There you are, potential corpse," said Christian. "And if you should happen to fall in and drown, leave word with your men to tell me right away. I hate to wait for a laugh."

Punjo's left eye jiggled sharply and he grinned a greasy grin. "Thank you, Mister Christian. Thank you kindly, Mister Christian. I 'opes you'll be comfortable 'ere, Mister Christian. I've got about five hundred men 'round and about in the jungle and they won't let anything get in to 'urt you none to speak about."

He put the paper in his moldy sun helmet, beckoned to the men who had carried the poles and withdrew, his court following him in all the brightness of their red and yellow paint. He was a Satan followed by hobgoblins, quickly swallowed by the jungle steam.

Christian motioned his hand at Hihi and Hihi promptly

began to cut the three loose. George growled something and it was seen that he dropped rather hard to the ground.

"Dear me," said the professor perplexedly. "Where did you come from, Mr. Christian?"

George stood up and rubbed his chafed wrists. George, it was seen, had sweat out a few pounds of his padding and he looked very angry. "Christian, wipe those natives out immediately. I won't stand for this sort of treatment. They made me sleep tied up and I've got a good notion . . ."

Christian looked queerly at George and noticed that George had said nothing about Diana's treatment or her hardships.

Diana had a scared look in her eyes as though all this was unreal and would immediately vanish, but if Christian expected immediate praise he was disappointed. Diana looked long at him as though he were something just as obnoxious as the headhunters.

"I suppose," said Diana, "that you have bought us off. What are *you* going to do with us?"

"Nothing," said Christian.

George repeated his demand. "See here, my good fellow, don't stand there talking. I demand that you do something as punishment toward these natives. If it's pay you want, I'll give you a thousand dollars. What? You won't take it? See here, my man, you can't make me pay any more and it's no use asking for it. A thousand dollars is the absolute highest limit. It shouldn't take any great amount of courage to disperse these devils."

"Is that so?" said Christian, smiling a little and looking all the way into George's soul without finding anything to speak of. "Then why don't you attend to it yourself?"

"Humph," said George. "I am a man of training. I am not a mercenary soldier. I am an anthropologist from Hale. An *educated* man has some rights and advantages, I'll tell you."

Diana frowned a little at Christian as though afraid of what he might do. Christian had a shining holster buckled to his thigh from which protruded the black butt of a .45 automatic.

"Well," said George, "go ahead. What are you waiting for? Certainly it cannot be that you are afraid of them."

"As a matter of fact," said Christian, slowly, "I am afraid of them. You are not free here, young fellow. Those jungles are thick with headhunters and we couldn't cut our way through if we tried. You are merely a prisoner upon somewhat better terms than you were before."

"Ah, so that's it. Perhaps," said George, "you wish to be bought off. I suspected that you were part of this plot from the first."

"George," said Christian, "you see those natives around that fire? Yes? Well, George, suppose you go over there and get some wood and keep the fire going for them."

"You dare to—"

"Go," said Christian with a queer little smile.

Muttering and frightened, George went.

Christian looked around and saw with a start that the professor was missing. "Where the hell . . . ?"

Diana looked all about her and then at the long house.

Christian followed her gaze and quickly approached the structure.

He heard the sound of footsteps within and he stepped to the doorway.

Moving under the rows of heads was the professor, picking up first one and then another and examining them all through a pocket glass he had somehow retained.

"Dear, dear, how strange. I can't believe . . ." He turned a head around and around, squinting nearsightedly at it and scratching his sparse gray locks with his free hand.

"I wouldn't do that," said Christian.

"Oh . . . oh, no, of course not. I say, Christian, look here, this fellow has a sort of odd shape to his face."

"Yeah," said Christian, stepping closer. "That's Lorenzo. I wondered what had happened to the poor devil."

"Um, how unfortunate," said the professor. "How unfortunate. I thought that this might give me the key I sought."

Christian went out and found that Diana was standing where he had left her, a sort of dazed, frightened expression upon her small face as she looked out at the overbearing, gagging greens of the jungle wall beyond the stockade. She looked at Christian and shuddered. He was part and parcel of the scene as far as she was concerned.

"A little too raw for her," thought Christian.

He found Hihi on guard at the gate and he stood there with the tall brown man for some minutes, watching the jungle wall, which did not move or change except for coils of steam extracted easily by the sun.

"Punjo Charlie," said Christian, "won't let us live very long, Hihi, after he finds that pool."

"No *sir*! Did you give him the right pool, boss?"

"I wanted to know where I could find him."

"We going to get out of here?" said Hihi.

"Tonight—late tonight. Hihi, I've got a pretty tough assignment for you."

"Nothing too tough for Hihi."

"Wait until tonight," said Christian.

He went back toward the fire and George glared resentfully at him. The coast men had entered into the joke and George was doing most of the serving, too, his eyes upon the trade machetes which lay carelessly close to the black hands.

Diana had found a patch of shade and sat in it, staring at her muddy, once fashionable boots, her face very melancholy. She looked so frail and tired, sitting there, that Christian was moved to approach her.

"Go away," said Diana, in a small voice, looking as though she was about to weep. "Go away."

Christian shrugged and walked past the long house. He could hear the footsteps inside and he stopped again at the entrance.

"Christian?" said the professor. "Christian, do you think I could take all these heads back to the coast with me? You see, a man by the name of Gregory published . . . Ummmmmmm, look at this, Christian. A Malay. A Malay! Now doesn't that prove that this race—?"

"His name was Dagger," said Christian. "He was Larsen's head man."

55

"That's too bad," said Forsythe. "I thought I had it at last, you see. Oh, well, here are plenty more to inspect."

Christian went back to the fire and sat down to eat breakfast. His head was spinning a little and he was heard to mutter, "A spoiled brat, a weepy dame and a daffy old man. Jesus, Christian, and you thought you were a barbarian."

CHAPTER SEVEN

The Trap Near the Pool

IT was a journey of several hours to the pool where shiny yellow gold still lay untouched in the riffles, ready for the first panner to clean it out. Punjo Charlie had to go there, find it, test it and then return. Christian knew that Punjo would be back the following morning to lead the attack upon the stockade and Christian wasn't waiting.

It was midnight and the whole world was black. No lights showed in the village and the fires in the jungle had burned out completely.

Christian stirred Hihi into wakefulness and bent over him. "You all ready?"

"Yes, boss."

"Then collect the others, and mind you, I'll hang your head in the long house if you make a single sound or let them give any warning to the brush. Savvy?"

"Yes, boss," said Hihi, sitting erect.

With another Polynesian, Christian went to the rear of the stockade and carefully unlashed a dozen poles so that they could be removed in a moment when the moment came.

Hihi brought the men and the packs into the open. He woke Forsythe and George and Diana and made them stand quietly waiting for Christian's orders—a difficult task.

"The idea," snorted George. "Making me get out of bed—"

57

A knife tickled George's fat ribs and Hihi's teeth were white against the gloom. George shut up.

The stockade was the scene of dismal waiting. The night was so still and everything was so black that you felt as though somebody had done you up in opaque velvet to muffle all sound and light and emotion. Men's spirits are low between midnight and two in the morning.

Christian found Hihi again. "All ready?"

"Yes, boss."

"Listen, Hihi, you've been pretty good to me."

"Yes, boss."

"And I haven't been too hard on you."

"Yes, boss."

"Then we part, Hihi."

"Yes, boss."

Christian took off his sun helmet and set it on Hihi's head. He took a shirt and a pair of white pants out of the packs and gave them to the tall brown man. Hihi donned them.

"Run like hell," said Christian. "Yell like hell and shoot like hell. You know where the pool is?"

"Yes, boss."

"I hope . . . I hope we'll . . ."

"Yes, boss."

Christian gathered up his men and the three members of the Forsythe "Expedition" and took his station at the rear of the compound, carefully removing the poles which barred their way.

Hihi was a white blur in the darkness, looking uncommonly

like Christian. He walked stiffly toward the front gate, rifle in his cool palms, quite as if he were going out to bag a jungle deer instead of a yelling mob of headhunters.

Hihi went out of the gate. A hoarse shout was heard in the brush. A bowstring twanged and an arrow whistled overhead.

Hihi started to run straight at the jungle, firing rapidly into the blackness from his hip, the exploding powder lighting up a round, orange globe of night.

More arrows, more shouts. Hihi bellowed profanely and wallowed into the undergrowth, still shooting.

Christian could hear nothing of Hihi's fate after that. The whole jungle came awake with a concerted yapping as though five hundred jackals were suddenly loosed.

Brush threshed, bare feet patted over bare ground. Hoarse cries of anger and triumph burst from the vicious throats of Punjo's pawns.

They were up and away and after the man who had been decried by the guard as the white man.

Christian's face was impassive, no matter what he felt. He wrenched the poles out of the stockade wall, regardless of the noise he made. Nothing could be heard above the bedlam in the jungle. He had the uneasy vision of a stag going down under the slavering fangs of wolves.

The sound was changing, much louder at the gate, completely abating at the rear of the stockade.

Christian trotted out into the jungle which faced them, followed by a long line of nervous humanity. Without lights, the natives hooked their fingers into one another's G-string and went like a long line of cars. Two Polynesians rode herd upon the professor and George and Diana and kept them in motion.

The cries were growing distant in front of the village. The unorganized, uncommanded mob of headhunters were all away from their posts, following the mass of commotion and the occasional rifle reports. After an interval of fifteen minutes, no more shots were heard.

Christian was sweating and found that chills were going up and down his spine as he walked. No more shots meant that Hihi . . .

They struck a trail immediately and sped down it, using the Southern Cross for direction. Christian felt his way forward, tripping across fallen branches and often going down in the slippery mud. He wished ardently for a flashlight but he could not have used it if he had had it.

They traveled for an hour and were beginning to congratulate themselves upon their escape when one of the coast men fell and refused to rise at his companions' insistence. Questing fingers found an arrow in his back.

Instantly the cry went up and a moment later the whistling song of feathered death mounted into full chorus.

Tracked, followed and trapped by men who knew these trails too well!

Christian threw the Polynesian into the lead. "You know where the pool is. Head for it. Fast!"

The Polynesian went and the line scuttled past Christian like so many black beetles running from a fire. The professor brushed past, carried on in the rush. George was gasping with fright and falling every few feet. Diana, in the starlight, cast a puzzled glance at Christian as she shouldered past.

The sub-tommy went into action, sweeping their back trail with long, raking bursts. The blossoming spotlight of red from the muzzle turned the leaves a sick color and caught in the whites of eyes behind them.

A mass of headhunters tried to get out of the path. The muzzle went back and forth, back and forth. The recoil shook Christian as though he experienced a violent species of ague. His mouth was relaxed and his hands were deft and efficient. He might as well have been shooting at cloth targets on a police range for all the expression he had.

The trail was emptied. Christian turned and ran, the air growing thick and loud about his head.

He whirled at the next bend and fired another burst. Once more he darted after the column.

He contacted the rear guard in the form of one of his men. "Faster!" cried Christian.

The line sped up and Christian waited in the darkness, again left alone. His khaki did not wholly blend with the night but the headhunters were excited and vengeful and they failed to see him.

A native ran headlong into the sub-Thompson's muzzle. Christian turned it loose.

Again the trail was lighted as though by a torch, again it was cleared and carpeted at the same time. The mud was slippery underfoot.

The drum rolled and shells rattled. The firing pin snapped on an empty chamber. Christian turned and caught up with the column again, loading from a musette bag as he ran.

The march proceeded with great alacrity. There were no stragglers, there were no complaints at the pace, only a few muttered words when a man fell and had to be dragged to his feet again.

An hour stretched itself out unbelievably. Christian's mind was filled with Hihi's fate. If he had done it himself, these people couldn't have been gotten out. But he should have done it himself. Hihi had no interest in these people. Hihi had a wife in the Marquesas and a thatched hut and a whole menagerie of animals he had befriended.

"Get along, you fools!" roared Christian, and felt like somebody trying to drive loafing cattle before a storm broke and wiped them out in a flood—a red flood.

George was whining about it being wet and nasty and occasionally the professor said, "Dear me." Diana had nothing whatever to say. She only trudged along with her fingers in a native's pack harness and tried not to give way to the panic which welled terribly inside her.

"Step out!" cried Christian, turning again.

But the natives had had enough. They had paved their trail—and perhaps a section of hell—with their fellows and they knew that there was plenty of time. The upcountry was too large to permit a stealthy escape. If not tonight, then tomorrow.

In the vanguard a rifle banged. The line piled up into a

scared huddle. The coast men chattered with anxiety. Again the report split the night with sparks.

Christian waded through the crowd, shoving men to the right and left. He came up to the Polynesian.

The brown man pointed with some pride at a headhunter who was trying hard to breathe through his own swelling blood, spread-eagled in the muck.

"The pool's ahead," said Christian. "Stay together and wait."

This he knew had been a sentry and he knew that the shots had long since alarmed whatever men Punjo Charlie had taken with him.

Christian left the trail and threshed through the underbrush toward the stream he knew would lie just ahead. He could see a spark of light before him and he knew that the camp was stirring. Shadows flitted back and forth before the dot.

Sliding down the bank, Christian splashed into water which gurgled strongly about his hips. He held the sub-tommy over his head and waded, hoping he would not strike a pool and go under.

The creek was narrow and Christian soon made the other bank. He quickly skirted the camp and saw the activity there. The natives were leaving as fast as they could get their weapons together, heading for the point where the shots had sounded.

Christian tried to locate Punjo Charlie but could not. All shadows were alike. Perhaps Punjo was already heading for the trail, gun in hand, his natives with him, not waiting for the rest of his men to follow.

Christian had no compunctions where the headhunters

were concerned. He stepped out into the open, yelled at them, and then cut loose.

He was like a fireman behind the nozzle of a pressure hose. The stream was red- and white-hot, and wherever he directed it, men were thrown down and knocked rolling, shivering and jumping with queer laxness.

A few got away and went hurtling up the trail after Punjo Charlie. Christian sprinted after them.

The rifle went again, signifying that Punjo had contacted the column. Another press of headhunters, bows and knives ready, waited for Punjo's orders.

Punjo's bawl could be heard in the jungle somewhere. He was yelling in dialect. The natives understood and swarmed into the trail to rush the column.

Behind them Christian cried out—not to give them a chance, but merely to make them hesitate long enough for the sub-tommy to do some good.

The spraying, leaping muzzle buffeted them, spun them about, threw them into queerly twisted piles which began to shine in the light of exploding powder.

"Come on!" cried Christian.

The headhunters tried to rush him and flank him. They went down like a line of dominoes, swiftly, without staggering or yelling or even looking up again.

The Polynesian and the column rushed forward, stumbling over the motionless shadows which blocked up the path. They headed with one accord toward the fire and even Christian's yell would not turn them away again.

But the coast men and the three white people did not make targets of themselves for long. With relief, Christian saw that Punjo had caused a small bulwark to be built about the camp in case another tribe wanted to attack or perhaps in case Christian got loose.

Although the earthwork had certainly done Punjo no good whatever, it made admirable cover for the coast men and the Polynesians.

Christian waited hopefully for a rush, a fresh drum in his sub-tommy, ready to spray again. So far he had had to deal with small parties. He knew that if he tarried there for long, the main villages would come up, if only for vengeance against him.

Punjo was out there somewhere, trying to rally his forces. Punjo Charlie, thought Christian, would do better if he thought less of his own cunning.

It was almost dawn again and Christian kicked the fire apart and stationed his men at convenient points. He searched along the earthwork for Diana and finally found her, huddled in a small ball, completely exhausted and sound asleep.

He smiled at her and shoved a pack under her head.

George was whining somewhere near at hand and the professor was calmly looking at the bodies which were strewn about the pulsating coals of the dying fire.

"Too true," said the professor. "Too true. They certainly look the type."

Christian looked at him in perplexity and then went back to the earthwork to make certain that no dawn attack would come off. If he could only do something to keep them from gathering in too big a force, they might be able to do their work and get out of here.

And again they might not.

The pool was close at hand.

CHAPTER EIGHT

Waiting for Attack

TOM CHRISTIAN still had a great number of coast men and they were still in great fear—especially when stray arrows clipped close to their gigantic thatches of hair. The coast men did not have to be told that the arrow points were so smeared that a man would die in horrible agony within the hour at a mere scratch.

It was thus with some difficulty that Christian made them go to work on the barricade, raising it until it was quite arrowproof unless some headhunter figured out trajectory by calculus and managed to drop a barrage of feathered death down in the parabolic manner of the Stokes mortar.

When noon came the place was fairly defensible. The headhunters had finally discovered that the sub-tommy was quite lethal and had a most unhappy habit of knocking men into battered hamburger without half trying. In spite of the fact that Punjo repeatedly removed and polished his glass eye and made all manner of weird sounds as though communing with all manner of devils, no concerted attack was forthcoming and Christian began to breathe more easily.

No one knew better than Christian that they were quite effectually trapped. The frowning ridges of the hills—with trees like hair standing uncouth and uncombed—were visible on every side. One pass was available but Christian was not enough of an optimist to think that he would find that open. It appeared, on the face of it, that the professor would get his wish about long houses and would have several centuries in which to study the heads of dead men while his own dangled happily in their midst by a string.

The stream, pouring over shallow gravel, had a laughing sound which, considering that Christian had given the headhunters a watery grave and had let them float to their brothers, was a most gruesome thing to hear.

The stockade built and its defenses arranged and a plan of battle carefully outlined to all who could be entrusted with arms, Christian went to work on the pool.

He and Larsen had already cut away one great bank, leaving a protected pit in which the men could work. It was fairly simple to divert the bulk of the water through a canal and thus leave the bed and the sunken copper plates reasonably dry.

The sticky soil had been loath to part with its gold and Christian and Larsen had imported pumps with which to drive a heavy stream of water upon the bank, washing it down into the creek where the heavier gold would sink and catch in the mercury-smeared plates.

It was night before everything was done. In the morning the cleanup would begin.

A very soiled Christian came back to camp. He was splattered from head to foot with muck, soaked through with water, and generally plastered with vegetable matter of various kinds. But he seemed to be in a very good frame of mind and he actually smiled when he addressed Diana.

"Worried?"

"Not so very," said Diana, glumly.

"Keep your chin up," said Christian.

He handed her a plate of food and would have continued the conversation while he ate his own if George had not appeared from a very protected portion of the earthworks.

"See here, my good man," said George, determined to be pleasant, "I've thought all this out and I've come to a very enlightening conclusion which I think it best to impart to you."

Christian looked at him, reminded himself that George was no longer using an English accent, and went on eating.

"I have discovered that the headhunters," said George impressively, as though he had just that moment returned from a long and hard and terribly dangerous scouting tour instead of from a comfortable bunk, "I have discovered that the headhunters are all about us in the jungle."

"No!" said Christian.

"Yes, they are. They are fully armed. I saw three groups of them go slinking off toward the stream."

"Is that so?" said Christian.

George looked at him suspiciously to find out whether or not Christian was laughing at him. He decided he was wrong because Christian wore a most placid look.

"I think," said George, dropping his voice to a hoarse and impressive whisper, "I think we're going to be attacked tonight."

"Tonight?" said Christian, startled.

"I have no doubt of it," said George, shaking his head wisely.

"George," said Christian, "perhaps you have figured a way to get out of here."

George looked at him strangely. "A way out of here?"

"Yes. Some way to get out and get back to the coast without leaving our heads in a long house."

George turned whiter than fat meat. "Good God!" he cried, starting up in surprise. "Good God, Christian! You mean . . . you mean we can't . . . we can't get out? That we're trapped?"

Christian nodded solemnly. "Have some dinner, George?"

"N-N-No, I . . . I don't feel very well."

Diana's face was a perfect blank as she watched George stagger away. She looked oddly at Christian and then went on eating.

After dinner Christian heard a commotion out at the gate and, unbuckling his .45, went toward it. The Polynesian on guard was suddenly excited. He threw down his rifle and whipped off the rattan bindings which served as a lock.

It was as though a man had opened the door of his house to admit a blizzard. Arrows stuttered against the poles, whistling as they came. Through them darted a figure which was bent over and running fast. This man came through the entrance like a football. The gate went shut with a bang. The hail of arrows stopped.

"Yes, boss?" said Hihi, looking very composed and saluting.

Christian stood looking at him for a full minute. Christian's eyes were a little bit shiny and his mouth opened two or three times as though he had something to say and then promptly forgot it.

"You better have something to eat," said Christian, slowly.

"Yes, boss," said Hihi and swaggered off to the fire, grinning as he went.

Christian climbed up on a mound and studied the jungle through a slit in the poles. His eyes went a little bleak as he looked. His head turned restlessly toward the hills silhouetted against a sky painted red by a maniac.

He came down off the mound and began to see to his men, making certain that they stood up for an all-night vigil. He sat down by the fire again and began to dismantle the machine gun with practiced fingers.

Diana watched him with sad eyes. She looked bedraggled and uncomfortable and generally wretched. But for all that, thought Christian, she was a very beautiful girl and he wondered what she would say if he suddenly reached out, grabbed her to him and kissed her. Probably look down her nose at him, added Christian ruefully.

She couldn't stand life unless she had a curtain of civilization between it and herself. She didn't like things as they were. She wanted breeding and education when she chose her man. Degrees, maybe, and money, but always degrees. Too bad, thought Christian. She was a nice kid, too. Still, there wasn't any reason why she had to look at him as though she were quite ready to believe that he could sprout horns and coarse hair and drink human blood or something.

Maybe, he thought with a start, maybe she objected because he had killed some of these headhunters. Maybe she saw his hands smeared red. Maybe she put him in the same category as a murderer or something of the sort.

But that wasn't any reason for her to object to him. For Christ's sake, did she think that head of pretty hair of hers would do better in a long house? Now if she—

"Attack!" shrilled Hihi. "Attack!"

Christian whipped the gun together, loaded it and sprinted for the gate.

CHAPTER NINE

Torches Light Battle

THROUGH the darkness came three trails of fire which shed a rain of sparks down upon woolly heads. It was an awful sight to behold, the way the shadows played upon the naked bodies and showed up their paint.

Christian mounted the stockade runway and looked down, ready with his sub-tommy.

The torches came on at a rapid pace, sizzling and sputtering and leaping. The intention was clear. The headhunters meant to set fire to the stockade wall and render the defendants helpless.

Hihi cried, "Killum! Killum!"

The sub-tommy roared, its recoil shaking the whole wall. Christian swept its blazing arc back and forth and the torches were flung down into the muck and sputtered there, dying rather more slowly than their recent bearers.

These tactics of night fighting, being somewhat foreign to the Melanesians because they so feared the devils who walk in darkness, puzzled Christian not a little. Punjo Charlie must have a terrible influence amongst them, to make them go against the customs of a thousand years' standing.

A spattering of arrows thumped into the stockade wall and quivered there, humming. Christian stepped down from his exposed perch and left Hihi on guard again.

"This won't be the last of it," promised Christian. "Look sharp."

"Yes, boss."

The remainder of the night was hideous with screams and shots and the death which sang so gaily.

There was little rest for Christian. He patrolled the walls, stopping attempt after attempt to touch flame to the barricade.

It was a long night and a dark one and when it was through, Christian's face was haggard and even Hihi had lost some of his usual cheerfulness. Hihi had had a rather long siege of it.

Drearily, Christian ate breakfast. A spatter of rain began to fall soon after sunrise and made the day as gray as Christian's spirits. The spatter doubled and trebled and began to roar and then was gone as swiftly as it had come.

The marching legions of silver lances were painful to feel, such was their force. When the drops hit the brush it was seen to quiver. Another shower deluged them and then a third.

It occurred to Christian that the rainy season was upon them and that if he wished to get out his gold he had better work with all speed.

It was with rather ill grace that he spared a half-dozen coast men for a task other than bringing up the copper plates from the stream bed.

Christian had them build another wall, made of soft earth, across the front of the hydrauliced pit as a second line of defense in case anything happened to the outer wall. Behind this he had their baggage stacked.

Thus they were effectually guarded from three sides by the

sheer walls of the pit and on the fourth by the newly erected rampart.

The rain deterred the headhunters from pursuing their plan of burning the stockade, but it did not discourage three separate rushes to attain the wall. Each time Christian, at Hihi's call, put the machine gun into good usage.

It was thus that Christian became a little more begrimed than ever, but even the powder stains, the muck, the water and the battering rain failed to take anything from his bearing. He looked as though he commanded at least a division instead of twenty coast men, four Polynesians and three whites. So it was that he revived their flagging morale.

The copper plates were deeply embedded in the sunken riffle box. The men slaved to clean off the upper crust of silt which hid the gold. Time after time Christian was forced to wade into the stream to lend his heavy shoulders to the task.

At last they had the sluice on the bank and the panners were ready to go to work on the gravel and black sand. They did so with a methodical efficiency, as though in this familiar work they forgot that their own homes were far away and that a large number of disagreeable hillmen surrounded them and blocked off any possible chance of escape. Not one coast man there, however optimistic, thought that he would get out alive.

But the pokes grew in size and the mud and gravel reduced in volume.

Diana, with a small show of interest, came once to the sodden bank and watched the work. But she expected to see yellow gold and this was not. The mercury was mixed with it, making a lead-colored something which was very heavy and very dull.

"I thought this was gold," ventured Diana.

"It's amalgam," said Christian. "Mercury unites with gold and that makes it look this way. It catches on the copper plates and . . ."

Diana wasn't really listening to him. She was looking at the frowning hills beyond them with a trapped, hopeless expression in her eyes.

Christian wanted to comfort her, but he saw no chance of it. He was afraid she would look down her nose at him.

Hands thrust into the pockets of her grimy khaki jacket, Diana walked back through the rain to the stockade wall and sat down heavily upon a soggy piece of canvas. Sometimes arrows thudded into the poles a few feet from her head and each time she shuddered.

The professor looked very satisfied with it all and even evinced a technical interest in the amalgam, and went so far as to display a surprising knowledge by roasting a few bits on a shovel over the fire to vaporize the mercury. He looked long at the gold which was left, but he was not thinking of what it would buy. He was thinking in geological terms.

George regarded everything with a sick look. He was quite ready to give up his head, convinced that it was already as good as gone. He mourned helplessly over it and shivered every time a skirmish made the jungle rock with yells.

At last the sluice was clean and the small canvas bags which held the loot were ranged in a long line, ready to be made into packs.

It then became apparent why Christian had so many men with him. Although it did not make a very large show as to size, the line weighed almost two thousand pounds. One ton of gold.

It was late in the afternoon when they finished. Christian went to the stockade to look at the jungle again. It was still raining and the stream was slowly rising.

Christian looked over his defense plan and found nothing wrong with it except that it would be untenable within twenty-four hours at the latest. To get to the second barricade—the pit—the hillmen would have to cross a rising river and then storm a muck-greased slope. Christian rather thought that they would try it at least.

He made a tour of the wall and shoved his head over the top a few times to get a better look around.

After a little, a voice came to him from the jungle and grew louder. He could not see the speaker but it was unmistakably Punjo Charlie.

"Owh, Christian! 'Ave you cleaned the pool?"

Christian didn't answer.

"Owh, no need of hiding the information," yelled Punjo. "I 'appens to know that you 'ave, me bucko, and thankee kindly for the trouble. I wasn't 'alf sure where you'd planted the bloody sluice. Thankee, Christian, an' is there anythink you'd like to 'ave said as your last words?"

Christian remained silent.

"And the young lydy," cried Punjo, "knows what a fine bloke I am, actin' so gentlemanly last time an' all. Give 'er my wery best, Christian. My wery, wery best, and tell 'er not to pine. I'll soon be smoothin' her troubled little 'ead while I sees yours decorate the long house—and ra't ornamental it'll be, too. You came up 'ere, Christian, for rewenge and for gold and mybe, 'oo can s'y, for the young lydy. Hi'm a big-'earted cove, Christian, and I think I'd better take all three, tyking excellent care of all of them, Christian, includin' your 'ead."

Christian still had nothing to say and the voice still came from the jungle, a wailing, insolent, deadly whine.

"And remember, Christian, that we'll tyke amazing care of everythink, savin' you the trouble and being nice about it. And I'm thinkink that it'll be a fine sight for to see you aswingin' back and forth in the wind. And there I'll sit wiv me kids about me awatchin' you swing and grin and I'll 'ave the hopportunity, Christian, twenty times a day, to thankee personally for all the things you've 'anded me. My love to the young lydy, Christian, an' tell 'er not to be too impatient."

Christian knew what was coming then. It came with a yell. He knew, in that instant, why these attacks had so far been so mild.

From somewhere, perhaps from Forsythe's supplies, the headhunters had gotten shiny axes which would do the thing their comparatively light machetes could not. The stockade was doomed.

From everywhere, like a wave coming up all black from the gray green sea, came the hillmen. They were painted red and yellow. Some wore hideous wooden masks. Some brandished spears. Some carried double quivers of arrows.

But all of them had a set grimace stamped upon their misshapen faces—and all of them carried death.

The four Polynesians were instantly up beside Christian, their battle cry almost as loud as that of the hillmen. The coast men rushed for the stream, forded it, and flung themselves into the protection of the second earthwork. The three white people retreated with haste, George leading with a championship sprint which sent the water flying.

Christian threw up the sub-tommy, but he knew it was little use. It was effective against three score but not three hundred.

"Get back," ordered Christian.

Hihi looked at him blankly as though he did not know the meaning of retreat.

"Get back!" roared Christian.

"No, boss."

Christian threw the tall brown man from the runway. "Get ready to cover my retreat."

The machine gun began to chatter, almost unheard in the din of battle cries which swelled up in rasping discord from three hundred throats.

It was as though a scythe had passed through wheat wherever the machine gun sprayed. Men went down in heaps but others came on. It was as hopeless as trying to cut off the Gorgon's head.

Christian could not hope to cover the three quadrants of

stockade which were simultaneously assailed. He heard axes hacking to the right and left. He saw poles cave in to display terrifying faces through the breach.

Christian looked back at the earthworks and the stream.

"As you sow," muttered Christian, "so shall ye reap."

And as he was sowing death, his meaning was quite clear. No use to stay there any longer. No use whatever.

He dropped into the compound and sprinted for the stream, and then he saw that he was too late. Hillmen were rushing in to cut him off on both sides.

He stopped and dropped to one knee and let them have it. They cleared, falling with unexplainable swiftness.

Christian rose up to run again. Another group dashed in before him. From the earthworks, Hihi's rifle was beginning to crack.

The machine gun rolled. Christian ducked a hastily swung war club and plunged into the stream.

Arrows cut the water to shreds all about him, but Hihi was spoiling the aim of the archers. Christian struggled up the far bank and was quickly yanked over into the pit.

Hihi looked scared. He was breathing hard as though he had run far. He looked Christian over as one examines a valuable painting for flaws. Then Hihi grinned.

"No scratch, boss."

Christian threw his arm toward the earthwork. "Get up there, you fool! Hold them off!"

Hihi went and joined his three fellows. The hillmen were trying to organize and gather the courage necessary to cross the ford. And there Christian's genius asserted itself. Whereas the stockade offered a wide front, the pit had less than twenty feet of exposed line to be attacked. And numbers made little difference there.

"With this machine gun . . ." panted Christian, whipping off the empty drum to replace it with another. "Ammunition! Where's the ammunition?"

Hihi stopped long enough to yell, "Square pack," and then went on shooting.

Hastily Christian rummaged through the packs and found the one he wanted. It was terribly light and a dawning horror chilled him.

He opened the flap and looked within. Out rolled several beautiful specimens of dried heads.

"My God!" cried Christian. "How . . . ?"

Forsythe rubbed his glasses very, very hard and coughed. "I . . . I . . . well, it was too bad to leave all those heads there when I needed them so badly and . . . and I thought I had better not throw out the food and so I took the boxes there and . . . I didn't look to see what was in them. . . ."

For a moment Christian stood up very straight and then something went out of him. He turned wearily and went back to the earthworks.

An arrow barrage was coming thick. One of the Polynesians, sighting carefully at a masked headhunter, suddenly jumped back to his knees, clawing at his throat. The arrow had gone all the way through.

Christian laid the man back in the pit as tenderly as he could and then leaped up to the top again and snatched up the rifle.

81

One of the Polynesians, sighting carefully at a masked headhunter, suddenly jumped back to his knees, clawing at his throat. The arrow had gone all the way through.

"Keep down," ordered Christian.

"Yes, boss," said Hihi. "Yow! Them fellah dead!"

The masked man whirled and fell into the stream and slid down, inch by inch, until he slowly floated away.

The rain came again and drew a curtain between the far bank and the pit. The arrows lessened as the bowstrings became damp and therefore useless. It began to look like there was some hope after all.

Diana screamed and Christian whirled about. Diana was pointing up.

An archer had somehow gained the top behind and stood silhouetted against the sky. Even with a weakened string his arrow had force.

A second man took it through the heart and fell backwards into the stream.

Christian fired in the same instant. The hillman looked like a dropped bomb, curving out from the edge and hurtling down, growing larger and larger. With a loud squishy sound, he half buried himself in the slimy pit.

Hihi looked insane. He whirled on the far bank and gave them a full clip, dropping three men. His companion was muttering something which sounded like firecrackers going off.

Again the hillmen tried to rush the bank. The three rifles crashed out almost as fast as the useless machine gun.

A great shaggy head struggled up the earthwork, machete upraised. Christian rolled sideways, trying to fire. Hihi drove his rifle butt halfway through the headhunter's skull.

The wave melted into the water and fell back to unite again.

Christian gave Hihi a slap on the shoulder and a crooked grin. "Okay, Hihi?"

"Okay. Knock hell outa them fellah now."

This statement, considering that the hillmen would certainly succeed at the first sign of darkness, was pure faith in Christian.

Hihi stared incredulously past Christian and Christian turned to see the object of the stare.

Diana had come up to the top of the earthwork and had lain down at Christian's side. She took up the gun of the fallen man and looked into its breech.

She met Christian's puzzled gaze. "Surprise," said Diana, in a humorless voice. "I was on a college rifle team once, but I guess that's all I ever got out of college that'll do me any good *here*."

Christian began to smile and then, suddenly, Diana was smiling. He touched her arm and gave it a shake.

"I couldn't," smiled Diana, "let you do all the work forever. I'm sorry, Tom Christian, and I want you to know before . . . I want you to know that I've been a fool. That ammunition . . . I know what you've thought of us, and I know how much trouble we've caused you. They don't belong here, those two, and I guess I don't either. I haven't got the right, I'm not good enough to . . . to lay here beside you and help you. But if I can make any amends by . . ."

Christian was delighted. Every weary line went out of his face and he said sideways to Hihi, "I told you she was the right stuff."

Hihi had heard nothing of the kind, but he beamed and said, "Yes, boss."

"I guess it doesn't take a college education to make a gentleman," said Diana. "I always thought it did, living near a college all my life. Now I see that . . ." She glanced back at the poor huddled heap of shaking fear which was George.

Christian laughed at her. "College degree? I don't know that a diploma would stop arrows, Diana. . . . Hell, no use kidding you. Seven years ago I graduated from MIT as a mining engineer."

Diana was somewhat disconcerted. "You . . . you're a strange man, Tom Christian, and I wonder . . ." She looked across the river at the ravaged stockade and saw that the natives were forming again. "Tommy Christian, would you mind too much if . . . if I kissed you goodbye?"

A moment later, Hihi yanked Christian back to his rifle, yelling, "Here's them damn fellah again!"

CHAPTER TEN

Death in the Pool of Gold

IT was almost dark now and the rain completed the dusk with its steady hammer. It was a dull and dreary place to die. There was nothing pleasant in the thought of being hammered down into the muck and mutilated.

The hillmen were convinced now that the machine gun was no longer in operation and they became very bold, capering up and down the other bank and yelling in a hundred pitches, like starved animals.

They evidently wanted something in addition to their present force. The front rank repeatedly turned and yelled something back across the heads of their fellows.

Christian had an inkling what it was. In the gloom he could see a white figure moving in their rear. They wanted their great medicine man to lead them and ensure their success this time.

They were calling for Punjo Charlie who had, thus far, managed to keep himself in the background. But that was all over now. Punjo Charlie had to keep his face with these people and if he did not, he too would die.

Presently the shabby, rain-soaked renegade came to the edge of the stream. Christian tried three shots at him but the light was poor and he succeeded in hitting only hillmen.

Punjo Charlie was laying about him with a loud voice in dialect. Finally, when the night had come with that sudden tropical swiftness present even on rainy days, the four defenders of the pit heard men slipping into the rising water, which came up to a hillman's armpits.

Abruptly the rain stopped and one of those fascinating equatorial phenomena ripped away the clouds. Starlight came filtering through, giving things and men fantastic size.

The whole stream was covered with bobbing native heads. Christian looked to his few remaining clips and began to fire. Beside him Diana was trying not to shake. On the other side Hihi was counting his coups with audible grunts each time he shot. The other man was doing what he could.

It was a slow, painful thing, watching that steady advance and feeling that nothing, not even a steel wall as high as the stars, would stop it.

The sky closed in again and after that the rain came with redoubled vigor, and all the light there was came from four rifle muzzles which exploded out of time, casting forth a plume of scarlet brilliance as a snake snaps out with his forked tongue.

Surprising how much light those explosions made—or maybe it was the darkness. By them, Christian saw a man who seemed to walk on the water, high above the bobbing heads. It was Punjo Charlie, riding the shoulders of his hillmen.

Christian tried to fire accurately but he could not. And then there wasn't time.

A wave of shadows came hurtling up from the stream. The four were flanked and fronted between the space of shots.

With a yell which ripped the rain apart, the hillmen swarmed over them. It was the end.

But Christian had one thought, one last duty to perform. He reared up swinging his rifle about his head like a mighty bludgeon, smashing skulls and chests and sending men crashing back into the stream.

On all that crawling earthwork, Christian's was the only spot which was clear.

He charged along the top, battering men down, sweeping all from in front of him, a raving tower of madness dealing death to the tune of a swishing rifle butt.

Suddenly Punjo Charlie's whites were vaguely luminous before him. Christian dropped the rifle and reached out with avid hands and caught the man to him.

"Jesus!" screamed Punjo, his throat in a vise, his head already wobbling.

Christian shook him and battered him and kicked him and then, with a mighty shove, thrust him backwards into the pit and tried to follow.

But the hillmen were closing now, war clubs and knives thudding and slicing.

Abruptly a new noise joined the fray. A high-pitched chattering, like metallic laughter, filled the air.

Christian threw himself to the ground. Somehow he managed to get Hihi and Diana and pull them back.

The crackling rataplan made the air swarm with snapping sounds.

A machine gun had cut loose to their right.

Natives screamed in fearful terror at this new menace. They

were swept backward into the stream, unable to understand why they went down and were spun about and smashed even before they touched the water.

The staccato clatter kept at it. The earthworks were draped in black. The water was churned and stirred by falling men.

Two small spotlights stabbed into the darkness, boring round holes in the rain, lashing up and down the pit like angry tigers' tails. On the far bank of the stream, hillmen were trying to run away. The flashlight caught them and the brittle, snarling reports began again.

For several minutes all was still and then the flashlights began to bob up and down as men walked behind them. The twin spheres of brilliance crossed the stream and labored up the earthwork.

"Hallo there! Hallo, I say. Anybody alive?"

It was Lieutenant Barry and a patrol of native police and a very hot machine gun.

Christian, battered and groggy, stood up. "Hello, Barry."

"Oh, hallo there, Tom. Beastly weather, eh?"

"Terrible," said Christian, and to Diana, "My dear, you know Barry. Hihi!"

A long silence followed the shout and Christian took a flashlight from Barry's hand and began to thrust aside the mounds of dead hillmen. But he could not find either Polynesian. Perhaps they had dived into the river and . . .

"Hihi!"

From the pit came a courteous, "Yes, boss."

The flashlight jabbed down and picked up the limp body

of Punjo Charlie. Hihi was kneeling there, grinning with satisfaction.

"You throw," said Hihi, "me catchum, me killum."

Punjo Charlie's dirty jacket was filled with knife slits and Hihi's knife was dripping. Hihi then went back to work and presently stood up, holding Punjo's glass eye. He wiped it carefully upon his G-string. He regarded it with a faint smile.

"Strong magic," said Hihi, tucking it into his pouch.

The flashlight wandered on and picked up the other Polynesian, who was trying to sit up, having connected his head with a war club and just now coming to.

George got shakily to his feet and recognized Barry. Some of George's dignity returned. "See here, Lieutenant, you must get me to the coast. I have a very important appointment in San Francisco. I'll pay you. . . ."

Barry turned away from him. "Well! I suppose we'd better move on to a drier camp, old chap."

Barry blinked at Christian and Diana as any well-bred Australian might. They had their arms about each other and were looking into each other's muddy face. Diana was smiling and Christian was saying something in a low voice and Diana was nodding eagerly, her eyes bright.

Barry turned away and found the professor upon the earthworks. The professor had a flashlight and his magnifying glass and when Barry looked, Forsythe had the head of a dead hillman in his lap, turning it one way and the other, inspecting it closely.

Barry looked rather puzzled.

"Dear me," said Forsythe. "I knew I was right. Yes, indeed, this proves it. Oh, Lieutenant? Do you suppose it would be improper if I took this man's head with me? You see, a man by the name of Gregory published a pamphlet . . ."

Barry looked back at Christian, yawned and sat down upon Punjo Charlie, that being the driest place.

"Any time, you know," said Barry. "Any time!"

Story Preview

NOW that you've just ventured through one of the captivating tales in the Stories from the Golden Age collection by L. Ron Hubbard, turn the page and enjoy a preview of *Tomb of the Ten Thousand Dead*. Join Captain Gordon, hired to fly a team of American anthropologists on an expedition near the Arabian Sea. All goes well until an ancient map leading to untold treasure is discovered and all academic niceties vanish—replaced by murder and bloody deception to protect the secrets of the map.

Tomb of the Ten Thousand Dead

I have been asked to tell this story a hundred times. I have only told it once—to the British government, when they were quizzing me about the slaughter of the Lancaster-Mallard Expedition to Makran, Baluchistan.

My part was a major one only because I was the only man who escaped with his life. And that was strange because I had no real interest whatever in the findings of this expedition.

I am a pilot. Let it suffice to say that I was hired by Lancaster, a professor in a small Midwestern college, to pilot the cabin job they had bought across these awful wastes.

The expedition was boring most of the time until . . .

Tyler lay on his face in front of my tent. The morning sun was shining upon half the blade of a dagger. A spreading stain welled out over his back. Furrows were in the sand where his hands had clawed in the last agonies of death.

I blinked in the morning sunlight, unable to realize that young Tyler was really dead. No one had any reason to murder him. He was harmless, good humored. I was seized with the awful premonition that I might be next. Something was afoot, something horrible.

I stepped over the stones and knelt beside him, looking

at the knife. In the silence I could hear his watch ticking, *clickety-click*. Funny that it was still running while Tyler was dead. Funny that a machine should outlast its master.

Dazed by the sudden discovery, I looked blankly about me. A small pottery container was lying on the earth beside him. I remembered seeing it before. It had contained some document Mallard had unearthed.

I put out my hand to touch the knife.

"Don't touch it!" a voice behind me cried. "I've got you, Gordon. I've got you!"

Amazed, I turned slowly and stared into the muzzle of a revolver. Mallard's hand was shaking and his eyes were cold. He had me covered and I did not know why.

He was a big-headed, narrow-shouldered man. He was the kind you see poring over ancient skulls and ancient pottery finds in museums. He was as dry as the dust of the bones he found.

"Put away the gun," I said.

Lancaster, a brawny giant with a black beard, came out of his tent and stood there, staring at the tableau.

"Look what Gordon's done," said Mallard in a shaking voice.

"Wait a minute," I cried. "What do you mean by that? My God, Mallard, I know you've been ill and that you're upset, but don't get the idea that I'd kill Tyler."

Lancaster's eyes were baleful as he looked at the dead man. "I think you did. You quarreled with him the other day. No use to try to lie out of it, Gordon. We've got the drop on you. Here, what's this?"

Lancaster stooped and picked up the vase. He looked inside. "It's empty! Damn you, Gordon, where's that map?"

This was all coming too thick and fast for me. I stood up. "Don't jump at conclusions, Lancaster. I know nothing about your damned map."

"He's stalling," said Mallard. "He knows what that map means. He knows we've come out here to find—"

"Shut up," barked Lancaster. "Gordon, you'll throw your revolver this way and you'll march into your tent and stay there, understand? We're holding you for Tyler's murder."

Our native guide, a Dehwar named Kehlar, shuffled out of the cook tent and leaned indolently against a pole. He had an amused expression on his face.

"You won't shoot, Mallard," I said. "In the first place you haven't got the nerve, and in the next place, if anything happened to me, who'd fly that plane out of here? I'm the only man here who can fly and if I'm killed, you'll starve in this desert. This place has swallowed up the better part of three armies. There isn't a water hole for fifty miles. Go on and shoot, Mallard."

I walked toward him, deliberately. I thought I had the upper hand for the moment. Suddenly Lancaster dived for me.

He was bigger than I was and when he hit me I skidded ten feet through the coarse sand. I lit with him on top of me. He started to let me have it with his fist, but I jackknifed and threw him away from me.

Mallard stood back, gun limp in his hand, an expectant stare masking his nervousness.

Lancaster flipped and came at me again. Sand spurted in tan geysers when he hit the ground beside me. He whipped one into my jaw and sent me reeling.

The ferocity of his attack was something which would not be withstood. His hands were great things, as big as basketballs, and when those knuckles struck they left a deep and heavy mark.

I tried to make my wiriness count as much as I could, but it was a losing fight from the first. I had to stand up and slug with him.

His fists came like cannonballs and each time he landed on my body or face, great, round lights soared up and exploded behind my eyes. He was standing there, letting me have it, and I couldn't get away. I tensed myself for one good crack at the point of his jaw before he knocked me out.

I let drive and connected so hard that it numbed my whole arm. He rocked on his heels and then crouched down. I struck again, furiously. Blood pinked his cheek.

He cuffed out with his hairy fist and rocked me into a pile of stones. I staggered up, stunned, and walked into his left. He sent me reeling again. I could taste hot, salty blood.

I went down into the swirling dust and Lancaster kicked me deliberately in the side. Mallard brought out a length of rope. They held me down and tied my hands behind me. Kehlar, unmoved, helped them carry me into the tent.

I spat out a mouthful of blood. "You'll have a hell of a time getting out of here without me," I raged.

To find out more about *Tomb of the Ten Thousand Dead* and how you can obtain your copy, go to www.goldenagestories.com.

Glossary

STORIES FROM THE GOLDEN AGE *reflect the words and expressions used in the 1930s and 1940s, adding unique flavor and authenticity to the tales. While a character's speech may often reflect regional origins, it also can convey attitudes common in the day. So that readers can better grasp such cultural and historical terms, uncommon words or expressions of the era, the following glossary has been provided.*

---

baleful: threatening (or seeming to threaten) harm or misfortune.

Baluchistan: former territory of west British India, now the largest province in Pakistan. It is a mountainous region bordering on the Arabian Sea.

bib and tucker: "best bib and tucker"; one's finest clothes. The term is from the mid-1700s: a *bib* referred to a frill at the front of a man's shirt and a *tucker* was an ornamental lace covering a woman's neck and shoulders.

bit o' muslin: a young girl, a woman.

black sand: a heavy, glossy, partly magnetic mixture of fine sands. Black sand is an indicator of the presence of gold or other precious metals.

blighter: somebody considered a source of annoyance.

brawny: having physical strength and weight; rugged and powerful.

cabin job: an airplane that has an enclosed section where passengers can sit or cargo is stored.

coaming: a raised rim or border around an opening in a ship's deck, designed to keep out water.

Cochin China: a region covering southern Vietnam. Originally part of the Chinese empire, it was made a French colony in 1867 and combined with other French territories to form French Indochina in 1887 with Saigon as its capital. It was incorporated into Vietnam in 1949.

Colt .45: a .45-caliber automatic pistol manufactured by the Colt Firearms Company of Hartford, Connecticut. Colt was founded in 1847 by Samuel Colt (1814–1862), who revolutionized the firearms industry.

conquistador: a Spanish conqueror or adventurer.

copra bugs: beetles that cause damage to copra, the dried white flesh of the coconut from which coconut oil is extracted. They are metallic blue in color, but sometimes have a greenish luster. They are 1/12th of an inch long (3.5 to 5.5 mm).

counting his coups: counting one's strokes; successful actions or triumphs against an enemy, from the French word *coup* that means "a blow."

cove: fellow; man.

Dehwar: a member of a tribe in the Baluchistan province of Pakistan.

dry: indifferent, cold, unemotional.

forty-five or **.45:** a handgun chambered to fire a .45-caliber cartridge and that utilizes the recoil or part of the force of the explosive to eject the spent cartridge shell, introduce a new cartridge, cock the arm and fire it repeatedly.

gangway: a narrow, movable platform or ramp forming a bridge by which to board or leave a ship.

G-men: government men; agents of the Federal Bureau of Investigation.

gorblimey: blimey; used to express surprise or excitement. It is what is known as a "minced oath," a reduced form of "God blind me."

Gorgon: in Greek mythology, any of the three sisters Stheno, Euryale and the mortal Medusa, who had snakes for hair and eyes that, if looked into, turned the beholder into stone.

ken: range of vision.

Kieta: the principal harbor on the island of Bougainville, the northernmost and largest of the Solomon Islands.

laying about him: striking or aiming blows in every direction. Used figuratively.

long house: a type of long, narrow, single-roomed building that served as a communal dwelling.

Makran: the southern region of Baluchistan in Iran and Pakistan along the coast of the Arabian Sea.

Malay: a member of the race of people who inhabit the Malay Peninsula and portions of adjacent islands of southeast Asia.

Melanesian: a member of a people native to a division of Oceania in the southwest Pacific Ocean, comprising the islands northeast of Australia and south of the equator. It includes the Solomon Islands. The Melanesian people primarily fish and farm, and supplement their economy by exporting cacao, copra (coconut) and copper.

mess jacket: a waist-length fitted jacket, worn chiefly as part of a uniform on formal occasions.

Micronesians: the people of Micronesia, a division of Oceania in the western Pacific Ocean comprising the islands east of the Philippines and north of the equator.

MIT: Massachusetts Institute of Technology; a private, coeducational research university located in Cambridge, Massachusetts. MIT was founded in 1861 in response to the increasing industrialization of the United States.

musette: a small canvas or leather bag with a shoulder strap, as one used by soldiers or travelers.

Negritos: members of any of various peoples of short stature inhabiting parts of Malaysia, the Philippines and southeast Asia.

not 'arf: not half; an exclamation of emphatic assent.

palanquins: covered litters carried on poles on the shoulders of four or more bearers, formerly used in eastern Asia.

panner: a container in which gold, or other heavy and valuable metal, is separated from gravel or other substances by agitation.

pith helmet: a lightweight hat made from dried pith, the soft spongelike tissue in the stems of most flowering plants. Pith helmets are worn in tropical countries for protection from the sun.

placer: to obtain minerals from placers (deposits of river sand or gravel containing particles of gold or another valuable metal) by washing or dredging.

poke: a small sack or bag, usually a crude leather pouch, in which a miner carried his gold dust and nuggets.

resident: Resident Commissioner; appointed by the British crown, they reside in the territorial unit they are in charge of. This was the case for the British Solomon Islands from 1893 until a governor was appointed in 1952.

riffle box: in mining, a long sloping trough or the like, with raised obstructions called riffles, into which water is directed to separate gold from gravel or sand. The lighter material is carried in suspension down the length of the box and then discharged. The heavier material, such as gold, quickly drops to the bottom where it is entrapped by the riffles.

riffles: in mining, the strips of metal or wooden slats fixed to the bottom of a rocker box or sluice (a long sloping trough into which water is directed), that run perpendicular to the flow of water. The weight of the gold causes it to sink, where it is captured by these riffles.

Scheherazade: the female narrator of *The Arabian Nights*, who during one thousand and one adventurous nights saved her life by entertaining her husband, the king, with stories.

schooner: a fast sailing ship with at least two masts and with sails set lengthwise.

sluice: sluice box; a long, narrow wood or metal artificial channel that water passes through when put in a creek or stream to separate the dirt and junk material away from the gold. Gold, a very dense metal, stays in the sluice box because of its heavy weight.

Solomon Islands: a group of islands northeast of Australia. They form a double chain of six large islands, about twenty medium-sized ones and numerous smaller islets and reefs.

Southern Cross: four bright stars in the southern hemisphere that are situated as if to form a cross and used for navigation.

spring holster: a holster that permits the user to take the gun from it quickly by pulling out instead of up.

Stokes mortar: trench mortar developed by an Englishman, Sir Wilfred Scott-Stokes (1860–1926). A mortar is essentially a short, stumpy tube designed to fire a projectile at a steep angle so that it falls straight down on the enemy. Pre-Stokes mortars were classified as "trench artillery" since they were not mobile enough to accompany troops. In 1915, Stokes designed a mortar that was small and light enough to be portable. It had a fifty-one-inch tube supported by a bipod, and the weapon could be broken down for easy transport. The cast-iron mortar bomb was three inches in diameter, and the Stokes mortar could fire as many as twenty-two bombs per minute with a maximum range of 1,200 yards.

sub-tommy: Thompson submachine gun; a light portable automatic machine gun. Named for its creator, John Taliaferro Thompson, who produced the first model in 1919.

swagger cane: swagger stick; a short stick or riding crop usually carried by a uniformed person as a symbol of authority. A swagger stick is shorter than a staff or cane.

van: vanguard; the forefront.

L. Ron Hubbard
in the Golden Age
of Pulp Fiction

*In writing an adventure story
a writer has to know that he is adventuring
for a lot of people who cannot.
The writer has to take them here and there
about the globe and show them
excitement and love and realism.
As long as that writer is living the part of an
adventurer when he is hammering
the keys, he is succeeding with his story.*

*Adventuring is a state of mind.
If you adventure through life, you have a
good chance to be a success on paper.*

*Adventure doesn't mean globe-trotting,
exactly, and it doesn't mean great deeds.
Adventuring is like art.
You have to live it to make it real.*

— *L. RON HUBBARD*

L. Ron Hubbard
and American
Pulp Fiction

B ORN March 13, 1911, L. Ron Hubbard lived a life at least as expansive as the stories with which he enthralled a hundred million readers through a fifty-year career.

Originally hailing from Tilden, Nebraska, he spent his formative years in a classically rugged Montana, replete with the cowpunchers, lawmen and desperadoes who would later people his Wild West adventures. And lest anyone imagine those adventures were drawn from vicarious experience, he was not only breaking broncs at a tender age, he was also among the few whites ever admitted into Blackfoot society as a bona fide blood brother. While if only to round out an otherwise rough and tumble youth, his mother was that rarity of her time—a thoroughly educated woman—who introduced her son to the classics of Occidental literature even before his seventh birthday.

But as any dedicated L. Ron Hubbard reader will attest, his world extended far beyond Montana. In point of fact, and as the son of a United States naval officer, by the age of eighteen he had traveled over a quarter of a million miles. Included therein were three Pacific crossings to a then still mysterious Asia, where he ran with the likes of Her British Majesty's agent-in-place

for North China, and the last in the line of Royal Magicians from the court of Kublai Khan. For the record, L. Ron Hubbard was also among the first Westerners to gain admittance to forbidden Tibetan monasteries below Manchuria, and his photographs of China's Great Wall long graced American geography texts.

L. Ron Hubbard, left, at Congressional Airport, Washington, DC, 1931, with members of George Washington University flying club.

Upon his return to the United States and a hasty completion of his interrupted high school education, the young Ron Hubbard entered George Washington University. There, as fans of his aerial adventures may have heard, he earned his wings as a pioneering barnstormer at the dawn of American aviation. He also earned a place in free-flight record books for the longest sustained flight above Chicago. Moreover, as a roving reporter for *Sportsman Pilot* (featuring his first professionally penned articles), he further helped inspire a generation of pilots who would take America to world airpower.

Immediately beyond his sophomore year, Ron embarked on the first of his famed ethnological expeditions, initially to then untrammeled Caribbean shores (descriptions of which would later fill a whole series of West Indies mystery-thrillers). That the Puerto Rican interior would also figure into the future of Ron Hubbard stories was likewise no accident. For in addition to cultural studies of the island, a 1932–33

LRH expedition is rightly remembered as conducting the first complete mineralogical survey of a Puerto Rico under United States jurisdiction.

There was many another adventure along this vein: As a lifetime member of the famed Explorers Club, L. Ron Hubbard charted North Pacific waters with the first shipboard radio direction finder, and so pioneered a long-range navigation system universally employed until the late twentieth century. While not to put too fine an edge on it, he also held a rare Master Mariner's license to pilot any vessel, of any tonnage in any ocean.

Yet lest we stray too far afield, there is an LRH note at this juncture in his saga, and it reads in part:

"I started out writing for the pulps, writing the best I knew, writing for every mag on the stands, slanting as well as I could."

To which one might add: His earliest submissions date from the summer of 1934, and included tales drawn from true-to-life Asian adventures, with characters roughly modeled on British/American intelligence operatives he had known in Shanghai. His early Westerns were similarly peppered with details drawn from personal experience. Although therein lay a first hard lesson from the often cruel world of the pulps. His first Westerns were soundly rejected as lacking the authenticity of a Max Brand yarn

Capt. L. Ron Hubbard in Ketchikan, Alaska, 1940, on his Alaskan Radio Experimental Expedition, the first of three voyages conducted under the Explorers Club flag.

(a particularly frustrating comment given L. Ron Hubbard's Westerns came straight from his Montana homeland, while Max Brand was a mediocre New York poet named Frederick Schiller Faust, who turned out implausible six-shooter tales from the terrace of an Italian villa).

Nevertheless, and needless to say, L. Ron Hubbard persevered and soon earned a reputation as among the most publishable names in pulp fiction, with a ninety percent placement rate of first-draft manuscripts. He was also among the most prolific, averaging between seventy and a hundred thousand words a month. Hence the rumors that L. Ron Hubbard had redesigned a typewriter for faster keyboard action and pounded out manuscripts on a continuous roll of butcher paper to save the precious seconds it took to insert a single sheet of paper into manual typewriters of the day.

That all L. Ron Hubbard stories did not run beneath said byline is yet another aspect of pulp fiction lore. That is, as publishers periodically rejected manuscripts from top-drawer authors if only to avoid paying top dollar, L. Ron Hubbard and company just as frequently replied with submissions under various pseudonyms. In Ron's case, the

A Man of Many Names

Between 1934 and 1950, L. Ron Hubbard authored more than fifteen million words of fiction in more than two hundred classic publications. To supply his fans and editors with stories across an array of genres and pulp titles, he adopted fifteen pseudonyms in addition to his already renowned L. Ron Hubbard byline.

Winchester Remington Colt
Lt. Jonathan Daly
Capt. Charles Gordon
Capt. L. Ron Hubbard
Bernard Hubbel
Michael Keith
Rene Lafayette
Legionnaire 148
Legionnaire 14830
Ken Martin
Scott Morgan
Lt. Scott Morgan
Kurt von Rachen
Barry Randolph
Capt. Humbert Reynolds

list included: Rene Lafayette, Captain Charles Gordon, Lt. Scott Morgan and the notorious Kurt von Rachen—supposedly on the lam for a murder rap, while hammering out two-fisted prose in Argentina. The point: While L. Ron Hubbard as Ken Martin spun stories of Southeast Asian intrigue, LRH as Barry Randolph authored tales of

L. Ron Hubbard, circa 1930, at the outset of a literary career that would finally span half a century.

romance on the Western range—which, stretching between a dozen genres is how he came to stand among the two hundred elite authors providing close to a million tales through the glory days of American Pulp Fiction.

In evidence of exactly that, by 1936 L. Ron Hubbard was literally leading pulp fiction's elite as president of New York's American Fiction Guild. Members included a veritable pulp hall of fame: Lester "Doc Savage" Dent, Walter "The Shadow" Gibson, and the legendary Dashiell Hammett—to cite but a few.

Also in evidence of just where L. Ron Hubbard stood within his first two years on the American pulp circuit: By the spring of 1937, he was ensconced in Hollywood, adopting a Caribbean thriller for Columbia Pictures, remembered today as *The Secret of Treasure Island*. Comprising fifteen thirty-minute episodes, the L. Ron Hubbard screenplay led to the most profitable matinée serial in Hollywood history. In accord with Hollywood culture, he was thereafter continually called upon

The 1937 Secret of Treasure Island, *a fifteen-episode serial adapted for the screen by L. Ron Hubbard from his novel,* Murder at Pirate Castle.

to rewrite/doctor scripts—most famously for long-time friend and fellow adventurer Clark Gable.

In the interim—and herein lies another distinctive chapter of the L. Ron Hubbard story—he continually worked to open Pulp Kingdom gates to up-and-coming authors. Or, for that matter, anyone who wished to write. It was a fairly unconventional stance, as markets were already thin and competition razor sharp. But the fact remains, it was an L. Ron Hubbard hallmark that he vehemently lobbied on behalf of young authors—regularly supplying instructional articles to trade journals, guest-lecturing to short story classes at George Washington University and Harvard, and even founding his own creative writing competition. It was established in 1940, dubbed the Golden Pen, and guaranteed winners both New York representation and publication in *Argosy*.

But it was John W. Campbell Jr.'s *Astounding Science Fiction* that finally proved the most memorable LRH vehicle. While every fan of L. Ron Hubbard's galactic epics undoubtedly knows the story, it nonetheless bears repeating: By late 1938, the pulp publishing magnate of Street & Smith was determined to revamp *Astounding Science Fiction* for broader readership. In particular, senior editorial director F. Orlin Tremaine called for stories with a stronger *human element*. When acting editor John W. Campbell balked, preferring his spaceship-driven

112

tales, Tremaine enlisted Hubbard. Hubbard, in turn, replied with the genre's first truly *character-driven* works, wherein heroes are pitted not against bug-eyed monsters but the mystery and majesty of deep space itself—and thus was launched the Golden Age of Science Fiction.

The names alone are enough to quicken the pulse of any science fiction aficionado, including LRH friend and protégé, Robert Heinlein, Isaac Asimov, A. E. van Vogt and Ray Bradbury. Moreover, when coupled with LRH stories of fantasy, we further come to what's rightly been described as the foundation of every modern tale of horror: L. Ron Hubbard's immortal *Fear.* It was rightly proclaimed by Stephen King as one of the very few works to genuinely warrant that overworked term "classic"—as in: *"This is a classic tale of creeping, surreal menace and horror. . . . This is one of the really, really good ones."*

L. Ron Hubbard, 1948, among fellow science fiction luminaries at the World Science Fiction Convention in Toronto.

To accommodate the greater body of L. Ron Hubbard fantasies, Street & Smith inaugurated *Unknown*—a classic pulp if there ever was one, and wherein readers were soon thrilling to the likes of *Typewriter in the Sky* and *Slaves of Sleep* of which Frederik Pohl would declare: *"There are bits and pieces from Ron's work that became part of the language in ways that very few other writers managed."*

And, indeed, at J. W. Campbell Jr.'s insistence, Ron was regularly drawing on themes from the Arabian Nights and so introducing readers to a world of genies, jinn, Aladdin and Sinbad—all of which, of course, continue to float through cultural mythology to this day.

At least as influential in terms of post-apocalypse stories was L. Ron Hubbard's 1940 *Final Blackout*. Generally acclaimed as the finest anti-war novel of the decade and among the ten best works of the genre ever authored—here, too, was a tale that would live on in ways few other writers imagined.

Hence, the later Robert Heinlein verdict: "Final Blackout *is as perfect a piece of science fiction as has ever been written.*"

Like many another who both lived and wrote American pulp adventure, the war proved a tragic end to Ron's sojourn in the pulps. He served with distinction in four theaters and was highly decorated for commanding corvettes in the North Pacific. He was also grievously wounded in combat, lost many a close friend and colleague and thus resolved to say farewell to pulp fiction and devote himself to what it had supported these many years—namely, his serious research.

Portland, Oregon, 1943; L. Ron Hubbard, captain of the US Navy subchaser PC 815.

But in no way was the LRH literary saga at an end, for as he wrote some thirty years later, in 1980:

"Recently there came a period when I had little to do. This was novel in a life so crammed with busy years, and I decided to amuse myself by writing a novel that was pure *science fiction."*

That work was *Battlefield Earth: A Saga of the Year 3000*. It was an immediate *New York Times* bestseller and, in fact, the first international science fiction blockbuster in decades. It was not, however, L. Ron Hubbard's magnum opus, as that distinction is generally reserved for his next and final work: The 1.2 million word *Mission Earth*.

> **Final Blackout**
> *is as perfect a piece of science fiction as has ever been written.*
>
> —Robert Heinlein

How he managed those 1.2 million words in just over twelve months is yet another piece of the L. Ron Hubbard legend. But the fact remains, he did indeed author a ten-volume *dekalogy* that lives in publishing history for the fact that each and every volume of the series was also a *New York Times* bestseller.

Moreover, as subsequent generations discovered L. Ron Hubbard through republished works and novelizations of his screenplays, the mere fact of his name on a cover signaled an international bestseller. . . . Until, to date, sales of his works exceed hundreds of millions, and he otherwise remains among the most enduring and widely read authors in literary history. Although as a final word on the tales of L. Ron Hubbard, perhaps it's enough to simply reiterate what editors told readers in the glory days of American Pulp Fiction:

He writes the way he does, brothers, because he's been there, seen it and done it!

THE STORIES FROM THE GOLDEN AGE

Your ticket to adventure starts here with the Stories from
the Golden Age collection by master storyteller L. Ron Hubbard.
These gripping tales are set in a kaleidoscope of exotic locales and brim
with fascinating characters, including some of the
most vile villains, dangerous dames and brazen heroes
you'll ever get to meet.

The entire collection of over one hundred and fifty stories is being
released in a series of eighty books and audiobooks.
For an up-to-date listing of available titles,
go to www.goldenagestories.com.

AIR ADVENTURE

Arctic Wings	*Man-Killers of the Air*
The Battling Pilot	*On Blazing Wings*
Boomerang Bomber	*Red Death Over China*
The Crate Killer	*Sabotage in the Sky*
The Dive Bomber	*Sky Birds Dare!*
Forbidden Gold	*The Sky-Crasher*
Hurtling Wings	*Trouble on His Wings*
The Lieutenant Takes the Sky	*Wings Over Ethiopia*

FAR-FLUNG ADVENTURE

SEA ADVENTURE

TALES FROM THE ORIENT

MYSTERY

FANTASY

Borrowed Glory   *If I Were You*
The Crossroads   *The Last Drop*
Danger in the Dark   *The Room*
The Devil's Rescue   *The Tramp*
He Didn't Like Cats

SCIENCE FICTION

The Automagic Horse   *A Matter of Matter*
Battle of Wizards   *The Obsolete Weapon*
Battling Bolto   *One Was Stubborn*
The Beast   *The Planet Makers*
Beyond All Weapons   *The Professor Was a Thief*
A Can of Vacuum   *The Slaver*
The Conroy Diary   *Space Can*
The Dangerous Dimension   *Strain*
Final Enemy   *Tough Old Man*
The Great Secret   *240,000 Miles Straight Up*
Greed   *When Shadows Fall*
The Invaders

120

WESTERN